The

Million Dollar Shot

The
Million Dollar Shot

Dan Gutman

HYPERION BOOKS FOR CHILDREN

NEW YORK

Printed in the United States of America.

First Edition
1 3 5 7 9 10 8 6 4 2

This book is set in 13-point Times New Roman.
Library of Congress Cataloging-in-Publication Data

Gutman, Dan.
The million dollar shot / Dan Gutman.—1st ed.
p.   cm.
Summary: Eleven-year-old Eddie gets a chance to win a
million dollars by sinking a foul shot at the National
Basketball Association finals.
ISBN 0-7868-0334-7 (trade)—ISBN 0-7868-2275-9 (lib. bdg.)
[1. Basketball—Fiction. 2. Contests—Fiction.
3. Wealth—Fiction.]   I. Title.
PZ7.G9846Mi   1997
[Fic]—dc21
97-6461

Reprinted by arrangement with Hyperion Books for Children.

Dedicated to the cool kids, teachers, and librarians
I met in the last year. I hope I inspired you
as much as you inspired me.

In New Jersey: Euclid School in Hasbrouck Heights, Delran School in Delran, Quinton School in Quinton, Strawbridge School in Westmont, Patrick McGaheran School in Lebanon, Tighe School in Margate, Kressen School in Voorhees, Winslow School in Sicklerville, West Bank Middle School in Paramus, Mary Ethel Costello School in Gloucester City, Good Intent School in Deptford, Riverton School in Riverton, Blackwood School in Blackwood, Van Sciber School in Haddon Township, Erial School in Erial, West End School in Woodbury, Indian Mills School in Shamong, Indian Hill School in Holmdel, Ocean Avenue School in Middletown, Hunter School in Flemington, Theunis Day and Kennedy Schools in Wayne, Beeler School in Marlton, Thomas Jefferson School in Turnersville, Christ the King School in Haddonfield, Hebrew Academy in Egg Harbor Township, Briarwood School in Florham Park, Greenbrook School in South Brunswick, Davies School in Mays Landing, Newbury and Taunton Schools in Howell, Thomas Paine, Joyce Kilmer, and Knight Schools in Cherry Hill, Glenview, Atlantic Avenue, Seventh Avenue, and Saint Rose Schools in Haddon Heights.

In Pennsylvania: Engle School in West Grove, Lauer School in Easton, Colonial School in Plymouth Meeting, Council Rock School District in Richboro, East Ward School in Downingtown, Gwynedd-Mercy Academy in Norristown, and Hillendale School in Kennett Square.

Also, Silver Lake School in Middletown, Delaware; Villa Cresta School in Baltimore, Maryland; and Hilliard Station School in Hilliard, Ohio.

Thanks to Philip Reed and Dr. Tom Amberry,
who holds the world record for making
2,750 consecutive foul shots.

Contents

1	Eddie "Air" Ball	1
2	Annie Oakley	5
3	Don't Be a Fink	13
4	The Contest	19
5	Good News and Bad News	26
6	The Messenger	34
7	The Secret	40
8	Something's Going On	55
9	A Strange Visitor	59
10	A Show of Appreciation	67
11	The Mystery Friend	69
12	Fame, Fortune, and Finkle	74
13	What If I Miss?	77
14	The Million Dollar Shot	82
15	Slow-Mo	104
16	The End?	106
17	Okay, the Real Ending	108

1

Eddie "Air" Ball

OKAY, LAST PLAY! Your turn, Eddie Ball!" hollered our gym teacher, Mr. Ianucci. "This is Eddie's shot, everybody!"

It was the end of the school year, and Mr. Ianucci was putting the fifth-grade boys through a basketball drill. He had split our class into two teams, Shirts and Skins. I always prayed to be on the Shirts because I'm real skinny and I don't like taking my shirt off in front of other people. My ribs show, you know? It's embarrassing.

But today I was a Skin. One of my friends, Ty Wegner, dribbled the ball upcourt. The Shirts backpedaled to defend their basket. Ty passed off to Johnny DeFonzo, another friend of mine.

As the designated shooter, I wasn't allowed to touch the ball until the end. The shooter's job in this drill is to move *without* the ball and try to get open so one of your teammates can pass it to you. It's tough, because everyone on the other team knows you're the one who will eventually take the shot.

I scooted under the basket and out to the corner of the court, but there were Shirts all over me. Johnny passed the ball to Ty. I cut back the other way, but I was still covered in the other corner.

"Okay," boomed Mr. Ianucci. "Pretend there are six seconds left on the clock!"

Oh, man! I *hate* when he does that.

I ducked behind Johnny, faked as if I were heading for the basket, and ran out near the foul line. I was open, and I figured I had about a second or so before I'd be surrounded by Shirts.

Ty whipped a pass to me. Quickly, I planted my feet at the foul line.

"Shoot it, Eddie!" Johnny yelled.

I took aim and put it up. The ball missed everything.

"Air ball!" Ty said disgustedly.

"Hey, we shouldn't call you Eddie Ball," one of the Shirts said, laughing. "From now on we oughta call you *Air* Ball!"

I heard the guys snickering as we filed into the locker

room. Mr. Ianucci slapped me on the back and said, "Nice try, Eddie. You'll sink it next time."

It didn't make me feel any better.

Let me get one thing straight right from the start. I can *shoot*.

I can shoot the daylights out of a basketball. I've always had a special talent for throwing stuff at targets. I can toss a soda can into the recycling bucket from across the room. No problem. I can fire a snowball at a tree across the street and hit it nine times out of ten.

It's like a sixth sense. Sometimes I set up a bunch of toy soldiers on a table and pick them off with a rubber band one by one. Other kids are amazed. I can shoot a bow and arrow like a laser beam. I'm always winning stuff at carnivals.

Of course, being a great shooter isn't good enough in a real game. You've got to be able to dribble the ball. You've got to be able to pass. You've got to be able to handle pressure.

I was never as good at those things. I get rattled when I'm playing in a game. The other kids are always shouting, sticking their hands in my face. Everybody's running around. It's all a blur. Too much pressure.

But give me a basketball and put me on the foul line with nobody guarding me. I can sink it. Like I said, I can *shoot*.

2

Annie Oakley

THERE'S ONLY ONE person in the world who can shoot better than I can. That's Annie.

Annie's last name is Stokely, but I call her Annie Oakley. Back in the 1800s, there was a famous sharpshooter by that name. I heard she used to put on shows where she'd shoot dimes out of a guy's fingers and cigarettes from his mouth, all the while riding a horse.

Annie moved into our trailer park last year with her dad. I remember it was Father's Day when I met her. I was feeling depressed because it was the first Father's Day since my dad died.

I told Mom I was going outside to shoot some hoops. She said okay. I think she was relieved to get me out of the way for a while. It wasn't *her* best Father's Day, either.

There's a rusted-out old backboard a few trailers down

from ours that hardly anybody uses. The net is all ripped and hanging by a string. Sometimes I shoot hoops with Ty or Johnny, who also live in our trailer park, but they weren't around. I was shooting and sulking when this African-American girl I'd never seen before walked over.

She was a couple of inches taller than me, but she said she was ten, like me. Her jeans were flopping all over, so I could tell she was as skinny as I was.

The thing I noticed right away was that Annie was totally bald. I mean bald as a lightbulb. I know some people lose their hair because of one disease or another, but this girl looked like she shaved her head. I actually thought she was a boy until she spoke.

"Wanna play a game of HORSE?" she asked.

"Sure," I said, flipping her the ball. "Your mom lets you shave your head?"

"I don't have a mom," she replied, as if she was saying she didn't have gum.

"I don't have a dad," I said. "Your *dad* lets you shave your head?"

"Why not?" she said, dribbling. "He shaves *his*."

Couldn't argue with that.

In case you don't know how to play HORSE, these are the rules. The first player takes a shot from anywhere on the court. If the shot is made, the second player has to try to make the exact same shot. If the second player misses, that player gets an H. Then the first player goes again. Any time you miss a shot after the other player made it, you get a letter. The first player to get H-O-R-S-E loses the game.

I don't know why it's called HORSE. It could be called CHAIR or SPOON or anything really.

"I'm not that good," Annie said before taking her first turn.

"I'll go easy on you," I assured her.

Casually, Annie sank a shot from the top of the key as if it were a layup. I went out there and drilled the same shot through the hoop. She popped one in from the baseline, and so did I. She hit a jumper from the foul line, and I did, too.

Man, this girl is *good*, I thought as I watched her set up her next shot. She was like a machine. On every shot, she did the exact same thing. First she'd position her feet carefully. Then she'd glance at the basket for just an instant. Then she'd slowly bounce the ball in front of her three times. Finally, she'd take another quick peek at the basket and put the ball up. It dropped through the hoop with barely a ripple of the net.

I don't like losing. A few beads of sweat gathered on

my forehead. I knew I would have to try hard not to try *too* hard. Because when you try too hard, that's when you miss.

"Where'd you learn how to shoot so good?" I asked her.

"Shoot so *well*," she corrected me. "My daddy taught me. He nearly made the pros."

"What'd your mom die of?" I asked.

"She got shot."

Annie said it matter-of-factly, but she missed her next shot after that. It was her first miss.

We were sinking just about every shot we took. Every so often one of us would miss and get a letter. I got an H, then Annie got an H. She had H-O, and then I had H-O. I missed a couple of shots to get H-O-R-S, but then she got sloppy and missed a couple of easy ones.

The game stretched on nearly an hour. I knew I would have to go soon to help my mom prepare dinner. Annie and I were both at H-O-R-S. The next one who missed a shot would lose the game.

Annie stepped up to the foul line and bounced the ball a few times in front of her.

"Okay, let's see you make *this* shot, hotshot," she said, glancing at the rim.

Then she closed her eyes tightly. She raised her arms and pumped the ball up without opening her eyes.

Swish. Nothing but net.

"How did you do that?" I shouted as I stepped to the line to try the same thing. I'm a good shooter, but I never tried to shoot *blind.*

Annie giggled as my shot missed everything. "That's H-O-R-S-E!" she shouted triumphantly. "Good game!"

I was too astonished to be mad that I'd lost. "You didn't even look at the basket!" I marveled.

"I *looked* at it," Annie said. "And then I shot it."

Annie explained that by closing her eyes, she's able to block out all distractions. She can focus in on what she's trying to do.

"But you can't see the rim!" I protested.

"I know where the rim is," she explained. "The rim doesn't move."

"I've got a little trick of my own," I said. I reached into my pocket and pulled out a shiny Susan B. Anthony silver dollar. "It's my good luck charm."

My dad gave me the silver dollar as a birthday present when I turned nine. After he died, I started carrying it with me everywhere. I know it's a silly superstition, but I feel like it helps me in sports and school and stuff.

"Whatever gets you through the day," said Annie. "Wanna play another game of HORSE?"

"I don't have time," I explained. "I gotta help my mom make dinner soon."

"Then how about a game of PIG?" she asked.

"PIG? What's PIG?"

"Same as HORSE," Annie explained, "but with a P-I-G."

I flipped her the ball.

When school let out for the summer, I found myself hanging around more and more with Annie and less and less with Ty and Johnny. I still liked those guys, but somehow I felt more comfortable talking to Annie even though she was a girl.

With Annie, we would start talking about something like soccer and the next minute we'd be talking about rowdy soccer fans in Europe. The minute after that she'd be telling me about some European king who chopped off people's heads and stuff. I never knew where it would lead.

But if I was talking about soccer with Ty and Johnny, an hour later we'd still be talking about soccer. And after a while, there's only so much you can say about soccer. I had to admit that Ty and Johnny were boring.

Here in Louisiana, summer is probably hotter than it is where you are. We don't have air-conditioning in our trailer and it gets pretty brutal in there, so I spent a lot of time outside with Annie. We played B-ball, caught frogs and fished by the creek, climbed trees and stuff. There isn't a whole lot to do around the trailer park. But summer shot by. Mom couldn't afford any expensive present when I turned eleven on August tenth, but she took Annie and me out for ice cream.

One day near the end of the summer I bumped into Ty and Johnny at the Quik-Mart and they looked at me suspiciously.

"Are you goin' out with that bald girl?" Ty asked.

Going out? It had never even occurred to me to "go out" with anybody.

"Of course not!" I said.

"You're sure spendin' a lot of time with her."

"Yeah, so?" I replied. "We're friends. You and Johnny spend a lot of time with each other. Are you two goin' out?"

It was probably the wrong thing to say. But the words spilled out of my mouth and I couldn't put them back in. Ty flushed and bunched up his fist like he was going to slug me. He didn't, though. He and Johnny just glared at me and left the Quik-Mart without saying another word.

They were just jealous, I guess. When Ty and Johnny saw me spending time with Annie, they must have figured I didn't want to spend time with them anymore.

And maybe I didn't.

By the end of the summer, I noticed they were going out of their way to avoid me.

One day I saw Ty coming down the street and he crossed over to the other side so he wouldn't have to talk to me. It seemed kind of silly and immature, but there wasn't anything I could do about it. It was sort of like an invisible wall had gone up between me and the guys I used to hang with.

3

Don't Be a Fink

EDDIE, GET UP!" Mom said, giving my shoulder a shake.

Ugh. The first day of school is the worst day of school. After sleeping as late as I wanted all summer, it was hard to get out of bed at seven o'clock.

Our trailer is tiny, even for a trailer, so Mom and I were bumping into each other as we rushed around trying to brush our teeth, dress, and eat breakfast. I wasn't complaining, but Mom kept saying this is no place for civilized people to live. We used to live in a regular house, but that was before Dad died. I combed my hair and Mom took a good look at me.

"I don't know how we're gonna do it, Eddie, but this year we get out of here," she said, holding my shoulders with her hands. "I promise you."

"Someday we'll be on top of the world, Mom."

I grabbed my backpack and dashed outside just in time to make the bus. A bunch of kids piled on at the bus stop in front of the trailer park. Ty and Johnny sat next to each other and ignored me. Annie was sitting by herself. She had a book on her lap.

"Whatcha readin'?" I asked.

"Dylan Thomas."

"Didn't he play for the Sixers?"

"That's *Isaiah* Thomas." She laughed. "And he played for the Pistons. Dylan Thomas was a Welsh poet. They're not related."

"Whatcha readin' that junk for?"

"Why do you read those junky comic books?" Annie asked.

"'Cause I like 'em."

"Well, I like poetry."

I had the feeling that Ty and Johnny weren't the only kids who thought Annie was a little weird, but I liked hanging out with her.

"Hey, are you and me goin' out?" I blurted as the bus pulled out of the trailer park.

"You and *I*," she corrected. "What do you mean, 'going out'?"

"You know," I said. "Goin' out goin' out."

"Well, we don't stay *in* all the time," she replied.

I left it at that. The whole idea of going out with a girl made me feel funny and I was sorry I ever brought it up.

The bus passed by the big water tower that had the words JACKSON—LAND OF OPPORTUNITY on it. What a joke that was! My mom says the only opportunity people have around Jackson is the opportunity to get *out*.

There aren't many stores or anything in Jackson. Just a lot of overgrown fields that used to be farmed and are now crowded with trailers and small shacks.

When the bus passed by the Finkle Foods factory, some of the kids hooted. Somebody spit out the window.

My mom works for Finkle Foods, and so does Annie's dad. In fact, most grown-ups around here do. Jackson, Louisiana, is what you'd call a company town. Mom says that if it wasn't for Finkle Foods, our trailer park would be a big meadow. And, she always adds, it *should* be.

Unless you live in Louisiana, I'm not sure you know about Finkles. They're these dessert cakes made of caramel, peanuts, and marshmallow. The whole thing is rolled in a ball of dough, fried, and then covered with milk chocolate. They're gooey and messy and you can still taste them sticking to your teeth a few hours after eating them.

I know a lot about Finkles because Mom runs the machine that shoots the marshmallow icing squiggles that decorate the top of every Finkle and Finkle Junior (which are bite-sized Finkles). Each Finkle has exactly six squiggled loops on it. Mom can decorate almost a half a million Finkles in a day.

Mom says she wouldn't eat a Finkle if her life depended on it. It's not that Finkles are bad for you (which I'm sure they *are*), but Mom says the Finkle factory is a terrible place to work. The pay is low, the hours are bad, and the work is really hard.

You can imagine what it's like trying to scrape marshmallow icing out of a gunked-up, clogged-up Finkle machine.

"If you hate it so much," I asked Mom one day, "why don't you quit?"

"Finkles pay the bills, Eddie," she said sadly. "And we've got a lot of bills."

I don't know how much money Mom has, but it can't be too much. Our car is always falling apart and she doesn't get a new one. I think Mom is still paying off my dad's hospital bills.

Besides, I noticed that people on TV who live in trailers are always poor. So I guess we must be poor. I would never ask her, though. In any case, I don't think there are many career opportunities for people who squirt marshmallow on Finkles.

Finkles aren't bad, actually. I was in a Finkle-eating contest at the Finkle picnic last year and I ate ten of them.

I threw up afterward, but I *did* eat ten and I won first prize—five boxes of Finkles to take home with me. Just what I needed, right?

The funny thing about Finkles is that it sounds like a silly made-up name for a snack food, sort of like Twinkies or Ding Dongs or Pringles. But the real reason it's called a Finkle is because the company was started by a guy named George Finkle.

The story goes that one day back in the 1970s, George Finkle accidentally dropped a bowl of peanuts, chocolates, and marshmallows into a frying pan while he was making pancakes. As he was cleaning up a glop of it, he took a taste. It tasted so good, he decided to sell it and call it a Finkle.

I'm not sure that story is true, but that's what it says on the back of the Finkle box. The company history is right below the slogan: DON'T BE A FINK! HAVE A FINKLE!

Anyway, George Finkle's face is on every Finkle box and just about everybody in Louisiana knows him. Soon, everybody in America would know him.

4

The Contest

AFTER SCHOOL ONE DAY in October, Mom came home and immediately headed for the sink to wash the marshmallow off her hands. She tossed a copy of *Finkle Facts* on the table. That's the newsletter that all Finkle employees have to read. I couldn't help but notice the big headline:

FINKLE TO GIVE AWAY
A MILLION DOLLARS!

The article said that Finkle Foods was sponsoring a big contest. The company had arranged with the National Basketball Association to have one lucky kid take a foul shot during halftime of Game 1 of the NBA Finals in June. If the kid made the shot, Finkle Foods would give the kid one million dollars.

All you had to do to enter the contest was send in ten Finkle box tops and an original poem about Finkles. The kid with the best poem would be chosen to shoot the million dollar shot.

"A million bucks!" I whistled.

"I don't know how George Finkle has a million dollars to give away," Mom grumbled. "Rumors are flying around the factory that sales are down and Finkle's going to fire half the workers. He should take the million dollars and use it to make a food people can eat without going into sugar shock."

Mom's a little bitter about Finkle, in case you haven't noticed. She's a pretty good cook, and a couple of years ago she invented a snack food of her own. It was a fat-free, home baked cracker with real fruit and yogurt inside. It was pretty tasty—and even healthy for you. We named it an Air Crunchy.

Mom took the Air Crunchy idea to her boss, who showed it to Mr. Finkle. Mom still has the letter she got from Mr. Finkle:

Dear Mrs. Rebecca Ball:

Thank you for your recent snack food submission. Unfortunately, Finkle has chosen to pass on the idea of Air Crunchies. Our research shows that Americans *say* they want healthy snacks, but they won't *eat* healthy snacks. They want marshmallow, chocolate, peanuts, and caramel. In other words, Americans want Finkles.

Thank you again for thinking of Finkle Foods. And remember, don't be a fink—have a Finkle.

Sincerely,

George Finkle

"Mom," I asked, "how much is a million dollars?"

"Let's say I give you a penny for your allowance on January first," she said, "and on January second, I double your allowance."

"You give me two cents," I said.

"Right. And on January third I double your allowance again."

"Four cents."

"Correct," Mom continued. "And let's say I keep

doubling your allowance every day. How long do you think it will take until you have a million dollars?"

"Sheesh, I don't know, Mom," I said. "Years, I guess."

"Wrong," Mom said. "You'll be a millionaire on January twenty-seventh."

"Get outta here!"

"Figure it out for yourself," she said, flipping me a pocket calculator.

Mom was right, of course. If she gave me a penny on January first and kept doubling it, on January twenty-sixth she would give me $335,544. The next day she would give me $671,088. Those two days together make more than a million bucks.

"Hey, Mom, can we start that new allowance system today?"

I was sitting in front of the trailer fooling with the calculator when Annie strolled over carrying one of her poetry books.

"How about a game of HORSE?" she suggested.

"Do you realize," I said, poking the keys on the calculator, "that if you put a million dollars in the bank today and earned 8 percent interest on it, a year from now you'd have earned $80,000 for doing *nothing*?"

"The trick is getting that first million," Annie said.

She hadn't read the newsletter. I told her about the Million Dollar Shot Contest Finkle Foods was sponsoring.

"Come on," she scoffed. "Nobody really wins those things."

"Sure they do," I replied. "They *have* to give away the prize or it's against the law."

"Believe me, George Finkle will find a way to weasel out of paying the money. No way he's going to pay out a million bucks for sinking a crummy foul shot." Annie's dad had told her all about George Finkle, too.

"Well, if I sink that shot," I said confidently, "he would *have* to pay."

"They'll probably get a million entries," Annie said.

"So I've got as good a chance as anybody."

"Yeah, like *none*."

"*You* like poetry," I said. "Why don't *you* enter the contest?"

"Me? Write a poem to promote George Finkle's poison-making machine?" Annie laughed. "I'd rather poke hot needles in my eyes."

Annie's a strict vegetarian. I don't think there's any meat in a Finkle, but she won't eat them anyway because of all the chemicals and preservatives.

"Did you ever read the ingredients on the side of a Finkle box?" she asked me. "It sounds like the stuff they use to make chemical weapons."

"Come on!" I tried one more time. "Enter the contest. It'll be *fun!*"

"Not even if they paid me a million dollars."

"They just might!"

So I was on my own. Annie read her book as I struggled to come up with something nice to say about Finkles. It was hard! This was the best I could do:

> Finkles ain't red,
> Finkles ain't blue,
> But Finkles taste great,
> And they're good for you, too!

"That's terrible," Annie commented when I read it out loud. I agreed. I was about to start another poem when Annie noticed some tiny letters at the bottom of the newsletter:

Contest is void where prohibited.
Employees, their families, and associates of
Finkle Foods are ineligible.

Shoot! Our parents worked for Finkle Foods, so we couldn't enter the contest. Disgusted, I ripped up the paper and tossed it in the trash. We went off and played a game of HORSE.

5

Good News and Bad News

WHEN ANNIE AND I hopped off the bus that Friday after school, we were surprised to see my mom and her dad sitting next to each other on lawn chairs in front of our trailer. They each held a can of beer. A few empties were scattered in the dirt next to a garbage can about fifteen feet away. Mr. Stokely is a really big guy, maybe six feet five, and he didn't fit into the lawn chair very well. He and Mom were just sitting there like zombies.

"Dad!" Annie scolded. "How much have you had to drink?"

"Not enough," Mr. Stokely replied with a burp.

"What are you two doing home so early?" I asked.

"We got downsized," Mom replied.

"Cut down to size," added Mr. Stokely.

"Downsized?" I asked. "What does that mean?"

"Fired," was all Mom said.

For months, Mom had been telling me about rumors that Finkle workers would be laid off. But when it finally happened, it took her by surprise. Me, too. Mom had been working at Finkle Foods for fifteen years. George Finkle gave her fifteen minutes to clean out her locker and leave the factory.

"Who's gonna squirt the marshmallow icing squiggles on the Finkles, Mom?"

"I don't know and I don't care," Mom muttered bitterly. "Probably some robot."

"How are we gonna support ourselves?" Annie asked her dad.

"I got savings that'll see us through the fall," Mr. Stokely said. "But I gotta get a new job. And it won't be easy. Come Monday morning, a lot of us will be out looking."

I felt my throat get tight. Then my eyes got watery and I realized I was going to cry. I didn't want to do it in front of Annie and her dad, but by the time I tried to stop myself it was too late. My shoulders were shaking and my chest was heaving. It was the first time I had cried since Dad died.

"It's okay, Eddie," Mom said, giving me a hug. "It's just a job."

"And a lousy one at that," added Mr. Stokely.

Once I started bawling, that set Annie off. She buried her head in her dad's shoulder and the two of us were crying like babies.

Mom sat me on her lap and wrapped her arms around me. That only made it worse, but it made me feel better, too.

"Don't worry about us," Mr. Stokely said, massaging Annie's neck. "Sometimes when a bad thing happens to somebody, it forces the person to make a change in his or her life that wouldn't have been made otherwise. And sometimes that change is for the better."

Mom tipped her head back and drained the can of beer. "Yeah, maybe we need a change."

She handed the can to me. I took a hook shot over my head toward the garbage can fifteen feet away.

Swish. Nothing but can.

I lay in bed that night thinking that I ought to get a job after school. Now Mom would need all the help I could give her. But there weren't a lot of jobs around here for kids. Some of them might be filled by grown-ups who were laid off at the Finkle factory.

I hate George Finkle! I thought, punching my pillow.

But at least one good thing came from Mom getting fired, I figured. Now that she was no longer an employee of Finkle Foods, I could enter the contest for the million dollar shot. The deadline was still a week away.

I took a pencil and paper out of my backpack and grabbed the flashlight under my bed.

What can you say about Finkles? I wondered as I huddled under the covers. They're gooey. They're chewy. They're kind of screwy.

In the morning, the flashlight was dead. I must have fallen asleep and left it on all night. But the poem was done.

It was sort of a rap poem, and I thought it was pretty good. When I saw Annie that afternoon, we went over to the old backboard and I rapped it to her.

Now my name is Eddie and my last name's Ball,
And when I have a Finkle I eat it all.
They're gooey. They're chewy.
They're absolutely screwy.
And when I go fishin' I use 'em for a buoy.
And just like a fish I can make a swish.

It won't be horr'ble
When I shoot for all the marbles.
Here's the scoop for the hoop—
I'll winkle and sinkle
And Finkle will pay me a minkle.

I looked at Annie. She rolled her eyes.

"You are living proof that white people have no rhythm." She laughed.

"Whaddaya mean?" I protested. "It's *good*!"

"When you go fishing you use them for a *buoy*?!" she imitated me, shaking her head from side to side. "What were you thinking?"

"I needed another word that rhymed with *gooey*, *chewy*, and *screwy*," I explained.

"You'll sinkle and Finkle will pay you a minkle?"

"That means I'll sink the shot, and Finkle will pay me a million dollars."

"That's awful." Annie giggled.

"I thought you *liked* rap!" I complained.

"I *do* like rap," she said. "But just 'cause you can make some words rhyme doesn't make poetry *good*. That's the worst rap song in the history of the world."

"Oh yeah?" I said defensively. "Well, if you think

you're so smart, let's see you come up with something *better*!"

"All right, I will!"

Annie took my paper and pencil and went off to the side of the court. I took a few layups while she worked, but mostly I just glared at her. My poem was great, I fumed. Who elected *her* queen of the poets anyway?

A few minutes later, Annie came over.

"Okay, I got one."

"Lay it on me, Shakespeare," I said with a snort.

She handed me the pad. This is what it said:

How could the Pilgrims e'er be contented,
When savory Finkles had not been invented?

"That's it?" I asked.

"That's it."

"Poems don't have just two lines."

"They can have just two *words* if the poet wants them to."

"What does *e'er* mean?" I asked. "Like Air Jordan?"

"No," she replied. "*E'er* means 'ever.' As in 'How could the Pilgrims *ever* be contented.' You know, like in 'O'er the land of the free and the home of the brave.' *O'er* is 'over' and *e'er* is 'ever.' "

"In what language?" I asked.

"In *our* language!"

This was news to me. "If *e'er* means 'ever,' " I asked Annie, "why not just write *ever*?"

"*Ever* is two syllables and *e'er* is one," she explained.

"Who cares how many syllables there are?"

"In poetry, it matters," Annie said. "Besides, *e'er* sounds a little British or something."

"Sounds a little stupid or something to me," I scoffed.

"Hey, don't use my poem if you don't like it," Annie said. "Nobody's twisting your arm."

With that, she stormed off the court and went home.

Annie can be stubborn sometimes, I guess. And nobody likes their poetry criticized. Not that it really mattered, of course. Millions of kids would be entering the contest. My chance of winning was so small there was no point in arguing over who wrote the better poem.

But after reading both of them again and thinking it over, I had to admit that my poem was pretty lame and Annie's was better.

I raided the supply of Finkle boxes my Mom had brought home before she was fired and I ripped off the box tops. I ate so many Finkles that I thought my stomach was going to explode. I ended up throwing a bunch of them at some bottles I set up on a fence.

I filled out the entry form, put Annie's poem in the envelope, and rubbed my lucky Susan B. Anthony dollar against it. Then I dropped the envelope in a mailbox.

6

The Messenger

YOU KNOW, I COULD keep you in suspense for a long time. I could tell you about the three million entries Finkle Foods received from kids all over the country. I could tell you about all the articles on the contest that appeared in newspapers and magazines. I could make you read a bunch of pages in this book before I reveal what happened in the contest.

I could do that, but I won't. That would be cruel. Besides, I'm busting inside. I have to tell you right away.

I won! I won! I won!

I *wooooooooooooooooonnnnnnnnnnnnnnnnnnnnnnnnn!*

I couldn't believe it when I got the news. It was the beginning of May, when the grass grows really fast. I had picked up a job mowing lawns after school. I had just come home and kicked off my grass-stained sneakers when this short guy in a suit and tie knocked on the door. Mom was out following up some job leads.

"Hi. I'm Mr. Otto from the Finkle Company," the guy said through the screen.

My first reaction was that Finkle was giving Mom her job back. But that didn't make sense. They wouldn't send a guy out to tell her that. I mean, we do have a *phone*. I'm not supposed to open the door for strangers, and this guy looked kind of strange to me.

"My mom's not home," I said through the screen. "What do you want?"

"Are you Eddie Ball?" the guy asked.

"Yeah."

"Well, Eddie," he said, pulling an envelope out of his jacket pocket, "here are your tickets to the NBA Finals on June 14. I hope you can make it."

It took a moment or two for it to sink in.

"You mean . . . ," I finally stammered.

"You're the winner, Eddie! You get to take the million dollar shot! Of all the poems we received, *yours* was judged to be the best. 'How could the Pilgrims e'er be contented, / When savory Finkles had not been invented?' That's brilliant! Mr. Finkle loved it! And he especially loved that a Louisiana boy wrote it."

The last time I won anything, it was a spelling bee in second grade. When it actually hit me that I was the winner and I would have the opportunity to become a millionaire by simply sinking a foul shot, I couldn't control myself. I started jumping up and down and dancing around like a lunatic, yelling and going crazy. That's when Mom came home.

"What's going on?" she asked, rushing to the door.

"I won, Mom!" I shouted. "I won the contest! I get to shoot the million dollar shot!"

Mom took the tickets from Mr. Otto and looked them over carefully. When she was convinced they were real, she shook his hand. Then she yanked open the door and gave me a big hug.

"You never even told me you *entered* that silly contest!" she whispered in my ear.

"Congratulations," Mr. Otto said. "We'll be contacting you to make travel arrangements once we know which teams will be in the NBA Finals."

"Boy," I said, "if my poem was the best, people must have sent in some *awful* poems."

"You know," the guy continued, "just about every poem we received was one of those dreadful rap poems. But yours was so simple, so dignified, and so

American. And yet, it sounded almost . . . British."

It *still* sounded stupid to me. But I wasn't complaining. Of all the kids in America, I was going to get the chance to take a shot worth a million dollars. The NBA Finals were a little more than a month away.

As soon as Mr. Otto left, I got a funny feeling. It wasn't exactly fair. Annie wrote the winning poem, I didn't. *She* should have the opportunity to take the million dollar shot. She should get the money if she makes it.

I ran over to Annie's trailer to talk things over. She and her dad were changing the oil in his car.

"Guess what?" I asked breathlessly.

"Your mom got a job?"

"Better than that," I teased.

"She got a job for both of us?" asked Mr. Stokely hopefully.

I showed them the tickets.

"You *won*?" Annie shrieked. "Of all the kids in America, *you* won that stupid contest?"

"*Somebody* had to win." I laughed. "I *told* you I had as good a chance as anybody else."

"Well, don't that beat it all!" chuckled Mr. Stokely.

Annie went nuts. She jumped up on the roof of the car

and started shouting, "Hey, everybody! Eddie Ball's gonna be a millionaire! Eddie's gonna be rich!"

"Shhh!" I said, trying to calm her down. When she finally did, I helped her off the car. "Listen," I said. "I wanna talk to you about something. *You* wrote the poem, not me. I want you to have the shot. It's only fair."

Mr. Stokely looked at Annie. He wasn't saying anything, but I kind of had the feeling he wanted her to take me up on my offer.

"No way," Annie said firmly. Mr. Stokely turned away silently.

"Annie, don't be dumb!" I pleaded. "This isn't lunch money. It's a million bucks!"

"I don't care if it's one dollar or a million," Annie insisted. "I'm not going to get up in front of thousands of people to help George Finkle sell his poison."

"He's gonna sell Finkles whether you help him or not," I told her.

"I don't care."

Like I said, Annie can be stubborn at times.

"Well, if I make the shot, I'm gonna split the million bucks with you."

Mr. Stokely looked at me. His mouth dropped open.

"I won't take the money," Annie insisted.

"Uh, maybe we should put something in writing," said Mr. Stokely.

7

The Secret

THE NEWS GOT AROUND school pretty fast. Mr. Ianucci was nice enough to let me use the gym anytime I wanted, so I could practice my foul shooting. There's a good backboard there, with a regulation rim and a full net. Annie and I biked over to school on Saturday for my first session.

When I opened the door to the gym, Ty and Johnny were in there shooting baskets. I hadn't spoken with them in a while. Annie was locking up our bikes to the bike rack.

"Well, look who's here," Johnny said. "The million-dollar kid. I guess you think you're pretty hot stuff now."

"Mr. Ianucci said I could use the gym at noon," I said as calmly as I could.

"Well, we still have two minutes," Ty informed me. "You know, Eddie, everybody knows you're a lousy basketball player."

"If anybody should be in that contest," said Johnny, "it should be *me*."

"Then maybe you should have *entered* it," I replied, "instead of sitting there on your butt."

"Hey, I can kick your butt all the way to Pizza Hut," Johnny said, pointing a finger at my chest.

I was about to take a swing at him when Annie grabbed me from behind.

"Forget it, Eddie," she said, holding me back. "You've got to practice."

Ty and Johnny fell all over themselves laughing as they walked out of the gym.

"Yeah, Eddie. Listen to your girlfriend." Ty smirked. "Time for practice."

"He's gonna need it," Johnny added. "Loser!"

"So long, Air Ball," Ty cracked as the door slammed shut behind them.

Let 'em laugh, I thought. *They* were the losers. Annie and I had the gym all to ourselves.

"Hey, Annie, watch this!" I said after we pulled a bunch of basketballs out from behind the bleachers. I put the ball behind my back, leaned forward, and flipped it over my head. It fell short of the rim.

"Very impressive," she said.

"Oh yeah, let's see you do *this*!"

I turned around so my back was to the basket. I bounced the ball once, and then kicked it backward over my head. It went flying over the backboard.

"Eddie," she said after I chased down the ball, "I think you should be serious about this."

"What are you worried about? I'm gonna make the shot."

"You're pretty sure of yourself," she said. "How about you take ten serious shots right now and we'll see how you do?"

"No sweat."

I stepped up to the line and put up a shot. It bounced off the back of the rim and came right back to me.

"That was just practice," I said.

"Tell that to George Finkle when you miss your million dollar shot," she said. "You're oh-for-one, big shot."

I drilled the second and third shots, but missed the fourth. Numbers five and six went in the net, then I missed seven and eight. I swished the ninth. Just before I let go of number ten, Annie jumped in front of me and waved her hands in the air. The ball bounced off the rim and off to the side.

"Hey, what are ya tryin' to do?" I complained. "Wreck my concentration?"

"Yes!" she exclaimed. "Eddie, you're going to be under incredible pressure when you take the million dollar shot. People will be screaming and waving banners. You *know* Finkle's going to try to ice you."

"I got ice water in my veins," I boasted. "I'll sink it. You can bet on it."

"Bet on it?" Annie sounded angry at me. "You just made five out of ten from the line. Fifty percent."

"Fifty percent isn't bad," I said.

"Eddie, on June 14 you're just going to get *one* shot! That's *it*! Fifty-fifty is not very good odds. And with the pressure on, it's more like forty-sixty. I wouldn't bet on you."

"Hey, lighten up, Annie. It's gonna be a piece of cake."

"Well, if you're so sure of yourself I guess you don't need *my* help," she huffed. Then she marched off the court.

"Annie, wait!" I called after her. "I'll get serious!"

But she was already on her bike, heading home by herself.

Now *all* my friends were mad at me. It was turning into a really lousy day.

Mom and I were finishing the dinner dishes when somebody banged on the door. We were surprised to see Annie's dad standing there, and he didn't have Annie with him.

"Come in, Mr. Stokely," Mom said, quickly putting stuff away so the trailer would look more presentable. "Excuse the mess."

Mr. Stokely had to duck his head down to fit inside. At first I thought he had come over to beat me up because of the argument I had had with Annie. But he had a gentle look in his eyes. And in his enormous hands he was holding a brand new top-of-the-line Spalding Official League basketball, still in its box.

"That's a hundred-dollar ball!" I said.

"You're right," he replied. "If you're gonna shoot your best, you gotta shoot *with* the best."

He opened the box, palmed the ball, and held it toward me. Compared to the ratty old basketball I've always had, this one looked like a ruby or an emerald or something.

"It's for *me*?" I asked.

"Yeah," Mr. Stokely said. "But there's a catch."

"What's the catch?"

"You gotta let me coach you—"

"Sure."

"—And you gotta get serious. You gotta do everything I say."

"Uh, okay," I said. "When do we start?"

"Now."

"Now? It will be getting dark out soon."

"*Now.*"

Mom nodded to me and I left with Mr. Stokely.

"Shooting a free throw is the easiest thing in the world," he said as we walked over to the court in the trailer park where I'd first met Annie. The court was lit by a single floodlight. "There are only four ways you can miss. Short, long, right, or left. That's it."

He stopped at the foul line.

"Okay," he said, handing me the new ball. "Show me your stuff."

I spun the ball a few times in my hand, put my right foot forward against the line, and popped up a shot. It went in, and I was pretty proud of myself.

"You're takin' a *jumper*?!" Mr. Stokely exclaimed. He acted as if I had just murdered somebody. "Whaddaya takin' a jump shot from the foul line for?"

"I always shoot foul shots this way," I said.

"You shoot a jumper when somebody's in your face," he explained. "Puttin' your body in motion only increases the chance that you'll miss. You don't *have* to jump for a foul shot. Nobody's guarding you."

"The *pros* shoot jumpers on foul shots."

"That's why the pros only average 66 percent. Eddie, a free throw is not like a shot from the floor. It's a whole different game and you gotta play it different. If you wanna make all your free throws, you take a set shot. Both feet against the line. Both feet on the floor."

"A *set* shot?" I said, wrinkling up my nose. "That's how they used to shoot in prehistoric times, back in the 1970s. *Nobody* shoots that way anymore. It doesn't look cool."

"How cool is it gonna look when you step up to the line for your million dollar shot and you chuck a brick?"

"Not too cool," I admitted.

"Well, all right then. You wanna learn the secret to shooting foul shots?"

"Secret?" I scoffed. "I just put the ball up. Where's the secret in that?"

Mr. Stokely shook his head and chuckled softly to himself. He removed his wristwatch, slipped it into his pocket, and stepped up to the foul line.

"What do you shoot, Eddie," he asked, "50 or 60 percent?"

"About that," I answered.

"The rim is eighteen inches across. The ball is only nine inches across. You could stuff *two* balls in there at the same time if you wanted to. So there's plenty of room. You got no excuse for a miss. You should shoot 100 percent."

"*Nobody* shoots 100 percent," I said.

He didn't respond. He just bounced the ball slowly three times. Then he glanced up at the backboard quickly and took a shot. The ball swished through the net. I retrieved it and flipped it back to him. He bounced the ball three times again, looked up, and swished in another one.

When Mr. Stokely drilled five in a row, I was impressed. When he hit ten in a row, I was *amazed*.

But he just kept going. Fifteen in a row. Twenty in a row. No misses. He looked like he was in a trance. *Bounce. Bounce. Bounce. Look up. Shoot. Swish.* Same thing every time. I'd never seen anyone with aim like that. When the twenty-fifth straight shot dropped through the net, Mr. Stokely finally broke his concentration and turned toward me.

"So," he demanded, "do you want to learn the secret or not?"

"I do! I do!"

"Well, all right then," he said. "You gonna do everything I say? 'Cause if you're not, I don't wanna waste my time on you."

"I will! I will!"

He took me by the shoulder and moved me to the foul line.

"Put both your feet right against the line, shoulder width apart," he instructed, pushing my body the way he wanted it. "You need to be perfectly balanced. If you put one foot forward like you do, that makes your shoulders turn and you might miss to the left or right. You feel comfortable?"

"No," I said.

"You will. Trust me."

He handed me the ball. I spun it in my hands a few times to get the feel of it.

"Don't slide your hands all over the ball!" he scolded, snatching the ball away. "See that little black rubber dot, the inflation hole? Make sure that hole is facing up all the time."

"What difference does it make?" I asked. "The ball is round."

"You'll see. Put your thumbs in the groove here and point your middle fingers toward the hole."

He gave me the ball back and I did as he said, pointing my finger toward that little hole where you stick the pin in to inflate the ball.

"Now bounce the ball three times. Don't dribble it. *Bounce* it slowly. You wanna get that blood moving through your hands and arms. Now, what do you do with your legs?"

"I don't shoot with my legs," I said. "I shoot with my arms."

"You think so, huh?" Mr. Stokely said. He went to the side of the court and dragged a lawn chair over to the foul line. "Let's see how well you shoot sitting down, using *just* your arms."

I sat in the rickety chair and put up a shot. The ball didn't even make it halfway to the rim.

"See what I mean?" Mr. Stokely said, taking the chair away. "You gotta bend your knees and use your *legs* to power the ball up. If your shots fall short, that means you're not bending your knees enough. Your arms should just be used to *guide* the ball toward the basket. Pretend your arms are fifteen feet long. Then you could just *drop* the ball in the hoop."

I retrieved the ball and did as he said, bending my knees and reaching out toward the basket with both arms.

"Now what are your elbows flappin' in the breeze for?" he asked. "Keep your elbows in against your sides. When your elbows are out, you're gonna push the ball sideways left or right. You want your hands moving directly toward the target, straight for the basket."

"It feels stupid with my elbows in," I complained.

"It'll feel stupider when you chuck an air ball in front of a million people."

Couldn't argue with that.

"Now we gotta work on your *head,* Eddie. What are you thinkin' about as you stand at the foul line?"

"I think about making the shot," I said.

"Wrong!" he yelled. "You don't want to think about *nothin'*! When you think, half the time you're thinkin' negative thoughts. And negative thoughts make you miss. Quick, what's the two-letter abbreviation for mountain?"

"Uh," I said, "MT?"

"Right!" he yelled. "MT. And that's what your head should be as you stand at the line. Empty. I don't want you thinkin' about what you're gonna do tomorrow, or what you did yesterday. Clear your mind. Focus on *right now.* What are you thinkin' about right now?"

"Nothin'."

"Good! Now look down at the inflation hole on the ball for one second. Focus all your concentration on it, like a magnifying glass focusing sunlight on a spot so hot that it burns. Just one second. The crowd is yellin' their heads off, but you don't hear 'em. They can't change the flight of the ball. Now look up at your target. What are you gonna look at as you shoot?"

"The rim?" I said tentatively. I wasn't sure of anything anymore, but that seemed like the only possible answer.

"No!" Mr. Stokely yelled. "If you look at the rim, you'll *hit* the rim. You wanna look a little bit *above* the rim. I want you to imagine a column of air, an empty space that curves up and through the middle of the rim. A nice high arc like a rainbow. Now shoot the ball through that column of air."

I took a few moments to visualize a thick round glass tube leading from my hand up and into the basket like a funnel. I took a deep breath and prepared to take my shot.

"What are you starin' at?" Mr. Stokely suddenly barked. "Don't *stare* at the basket. It ain't goin' nowhere. Your most accurate view of a target is the instant you first see it. The longer you stare at it, the more you start calcu-latin' how far away it is and how high your arc should be.

Stare at the inflation hole. Then just glance at the basket. Your instincts and muscle memory'll tell you the right distance and direction."

It was a lot to remember. I stepped to the line again.

"Okay, Eddie," Mr. Stokely said. "It's just you, the basket, and the ball. Put it all together."

I took a couple of deep breaths and put my feet square to the line. I bounced the ball slowly three times, keeping the inflation hole up. I put my thumbs in the groove. Elbows in. Knees bent. Focused on the inflation hole. Glanced a little bit above the rim. And I put it up.

Swish.

"Now *that's* the way you shoot a free throw!" Mr. Stokely said, clapping me on the back.

"Wow!" was all I could say. It was an amazing feeling. It was totally effortless. I felt completely comfortable at the line. It felt like my body was a machine, engineered to do nothing but shoot free throws.

"Now do it again," Mr. Stokely said after flipping me the ball. "You've got to use the same exact routine every time you shoot until it's so repetitive it comes naturally. Like breathing. You'll get to the point where you know the ball's gonna go in as soon as it leaves your fingertips."

I did it again, and the ball swished through the net.

And again. And again. I drilled ten in a row without even touching the rim.

"How does it feel?" Mr. Stokely asked.

"Like a million bucks," I said. We both laughed.

"Now you know the secret."

The sun had completely disappeared from the sky, replaced by a show of stars. Mr. Stokely sat down on the blacktop, stretching his long legs out in front of him. I sat down too.

"Who taught *you* the secret?" I asked.

"My coach at St. John's," he said.

"Annie told me you almost made it to the pros."

"Came close," he sighed. "I was the star of the team my senior year. Averaged eighteen points a game. Scouts from the Lakers and Rockets were comin' around, lookin' me over. I was sure they were gonna draft me. I figured I'd be doin' my own sneaker commercials, drivin' a fine car . . ."

"What went wrong?"

"I got cocky. I goofed off. Didn't show up for classes. Didn't run my laps. Got lazy. I was so sure they were gonna draft me, I was out spending the bonus money I didn't have yet when I should have been practicing. Then I didn't get drafted. I coulda been with the Lakers. Instead I wound up with . . . Finkle."

Mr. Stokely spit on the blacktop, stood up, and extended his long arm to help me up.

"Sometimes you get one chance in life, Eddie," he said as he walked me back to my trailer. "One shot. No do-overs. This is *your* shot. Your opportunity to get out of this dump. Don't blow it like I did."

I watched as he walked slowly back to his trailer.

8

Something's Going On

THE NEXT DAY AFTER school, I *begged* Annie to go to the gym to help me practice. Reluctantly, she agreed.

"Watch this!" I said when I got to the foul line. Then I pumped up one hundred shots without stopping, making ninety-one of them. No trick shots. No fooling around.

"Well!" Annie said, a big smile on her face. "What's gotten into *you*? I like your new work ethic!"

"Your dad is a very good coach," I replied.

It was three weeks before the big day, and I started practicing seriously. Mr. Stokely had instructed me to take five hundred foul shots a day to improve my "muscle memory," as he called it. After a few days of that, I started shooting free throws in my head. Lying in bed at night, I didn't count sheep. I counted basketballs swishing through nets.

Annie was my main coach after school. Whenever my mom or Mr. Stokely weren't out job hunting, they'd come over to the school gym, too. Mostly they just watched, but every so often Mr. Stokely would give me a little tip.

"Don't be straight up and down, Eddie," he'd say. "You want to lean forward a bit. That puts you a little closer to the target."

One day, I was shooting my fourth set of one hundred shots and I was really in the groove. I had drilled something like eighteen in a row. Mom and Mr. Stokely had stepped outside for some fresh air. Annie was rebounding and feeding me the ball.

"Hey, Eddie," she asked. "Do you think something's going on between my dad and your mom?"

"Whaddaya mean goin' on?"

"You know. Going on going on."

"Nah!" I said. I put up the next shot and it bounced off the rim. I couldn't imagine my mom having a boyfriend. She hadn't been out on a date since my dad died. I hadn't so much as seen her hold hands with Mr. Stokely. I didn't like the idea.

"You notice she calls him Bobby now instead of Mr. Stokely?" Annie pointed out. "And he calls her Becky?"

"Those are their *names*!" I said. "What else should they call each other? You're nuts!"

"Don't you notice she laughs a little too hard even when he says the least little funny thing?" Annie said. "And when they talk to each other, they look at each other a *little* longer than they have to. It's like they're trying to see into each other's souls."

"Oh, man," I said. "You read too much poetry."

"I think it's cute." Annie giggled.

"Doesn't it bother you to think your dad might be going out with somebody?" I asked. "What would your mom think?"

"I wouldn't know," Annie replied. "She died when I was two."

I would have asked her more about it, but my mom and Mr. Stokely came back in the gym to watch me shoot my last set of one hundred.

With all the practice, I was shooting a consistent 90 percent from the line. In other words, I was making about nine out of ten shots, ninety out of a hundred. Hardly anybody can do that, including professional basketball players. Word must have been getting around about me, because people were starting to gather to watch me practice.

A funny thing happened at one of these practice sessions. I was standing at the foul line in the gym. I had just swished twelve in a row. Mom was next to me. Suddenly, from the corner of my eye, I noticed a guy sitting by himself in the top row of the bleachers. He was pointing a camcorder at me.

"Hey, Mom, who's that?"

As I pointed in the direction of the guy, he quickly got up and ran out of the gym.

9

A Strange Visitor

CONGRATULATIONS, EDDIE! How about a Finkle?"

When the famous George Finkle showed up at the door that Saturday morning, it was the biggest news to hit the trailer park in years. A real millionaire coming to call on *me*! A bunch of people from the neighboring trailers gathered around, craning their necks to see what George Finkle looked like in person.

He was a big man. Well, *enormous* is more like it. George Finkle was short, but he must have weighed three hundred pounds or more. I wondered how many Finkles he'd eaten in his lifetime. He actually *looked* like a giant Finkle.

The picture on the box makes it look like he's got a full head of hair, but in person he's almost bald. He's got a few stringy hairs, which he sweeps across his head. But it's like trying to cover a basketball court with a bunch of T-shirts.

He pulled a Finkle out of his jacket pocket. It wasn't wrapped in cellophane, like the ones you buy in the box. He must have lined his pocket with plastic or something so the grease and Finkle goop wouldn't get all over his clothes.

It occurred to me that this guy must carry pockets full of Finkles wherever he goes.

"No thanks, Mr. Finkle." I hadn't even eaten my breakfast yet, and the thought of eating a Finkle at eight o'clock in the morning made my stomach feel funny.

"Oh, come on, Eddie. Don't be a fink! Have a Finkle!"

"No, really. I'm full. I just ate breakfast," I lied.

"A Finkle Junior, then?"

Mom suddenly stepped between me and Mr. Finkle, her arms crossed in front of her.

"He said he doesn't *want* it," Mom informed Finkle.

"You must be Eddie's mother!" Finkle said cheerfully, stuffing the Finkle in his mouth and grabbing Mom's hand to shake it. "You're just as beautiful as Eddie is handsome."

As Mom reluctantly shook Finkle's hand, he leaned closer to her and said softly, "I understand you used to work for my company, Mrs. Ball. I just want to tell you I'm sorry I had to terminate so many employees recently."

"Business is business," Mom said grimly. "You gotta do what you gotta do."

"That's right," Finkle said, brightening again. "And if your boy, Eddie, here sinks his foul shot, maybe he'll use the million dollars to set you up in a business of your *own*!"

"If Eddie wins," Mom said seriously, "he'll put some money away for college. The rest will be his money to do with what he wishes."

Mr. Finkle had come with a whole bunch of people— a camera crew, reporters, even some bodyguards. I guess millions of people love George Finkle, but lots of others hate him—especially people he'd just fired. I heard some hissing and hooting from the crowd outside the trailer.

As the cameras clicked away, Mr. Finkle presented me with a sweatshirt with the word FINKLE in huge letters on it. "Save it for the NBA Finals," he advised. "You don't want to get it Finkled—I mean wrinkled."

He let out a big laugh. I let out a little one to be polite. Mom just grunted.

When the photographers were finished, Mr. Finkle pulled me aside and asked if we could have a few words in private. I looked to Mom and she said it was okay.

Mr. Finkle wrapped an arm around me and guided me

down the dirt path away from the people surrounding our trailer.

"I wanted to wish you good luck, Eddie," he said. "But I don't think you'll need it. I hear you're a very good shooter."

"I'm not bad," I said. It occurred to me that the guy who had been camcording me in practice was probably one of Finkle's flunkies. George Finkle was spying on me to see if I was any good.

"You're modest, too," Finkle continued. "I like that. Tell me, Eddie. Did you ever play ball with a lot of people watching?"

"No."

"The TV people tell me there may be as many as fifty million viewers watching at home when you take your shot," he said. "Does that make you feel a little nervous, Eddie?"

"A little, I guess."

"Well, I want you to know that if you miss the shot, I won't let you go home empty-handed. Hit it or miss it, I'm going to give you a lifetime supply of Finkles."

"Gee, thanks, Mr. Finkle."

It occurred to me that if I ate too many Finkles, my lifetime wouldn't last very long at all.

"Eddie, can you keep a secret?" he asked seriously.

"Sure."

"Will you promise that what we're about to discuss will remain just between you and me?"

"Sure, Mr. Finkle."

"Eddie, the Food and Drug Administration has been conducting tests on Finkles. They fed Finkles to a bunch of laboratory rats, and some of them apparently got cancer."

"Gee, that's terrible," I said.

"Yes, it is. The FDA might force me to take out some of the chemicals I put in Finkles that make them taste so good. When this report is released to the public next month, it will be very bad for my company."

"Not to mention all the people and rats who might get sick or die from eating Finkles," I added.

"Of course," he said dismissively. "Them, too. You know, Eddie, a million dollars is a lot of money, even to a man like me. I got in a little over my head with this contest, I admit. If I have to give you a million dollars, it will put me in an even deeper financial hole. Do you understand what I'm trying to say?"

"No," I answered honestly.

"Let me put it this way, Eddie. There's a little something you can do for me and a big something I want to do for you and your Mom."

"What do you want to do for me?"

"I want to give your Mom her job back, with a nice raise, too."

"Great," I said. "What do you want me to do for you?"

"Eddie," he said, looking me in the eyes. "I want you to miss the shot."

"*Miss* it?" I said, flabbergasted. I stopped walking. "You mean, miss it on *purpose*?"

"Bounce it off the rim, throw an air ball. It doesn't matter. As long as that ball doesn't end up in the basket, I'll give your Mom back the job she did so well."

That really floored me. I wanted Mom to have her job back, of course. But missing the shot on purpose! It didn't feel right. It seemed un-American, or something.

I asked Mr. Finkle if I could think it over, and he said that would be fine. He gave me a card with his private phone number on it. He said to call as soon as I made up my mind.

"Remember, Eddie," Finkle said as we headed back to the trailer, "what we discussed is just between the two of us, right?"

"Right."

Finkle and his entourage packed up their gear and left quickly, followed by some people calling out rude comments to him. When all the gawkers were gone, Mom asked me what Finkle had said to me in private. I simply told her that Finkle wished me good luck.

"Good luck?" Mom snorted. "That's the *last* thing he wants you to have."

As I lay in bed that night, I thought it over. If I missed the shot on purpose, I wouldn't have a million dollars, but my mom would get her job back and we'd be back to normal.

Then I thought it over some more. If I missed the shot on purpose, for the rest of my life I would be thinking that I gave up the chance to make an easy million dollars.

And then I thought it over some more. If I *made* the shot, I'd get a million dollars and Finkle Foods would probably go out of business. Mom wouldn't get her job back, of course. But if we had a million dollars she wouldn't *need* her job back.

And who knows how many people I might save by driving Finkle out of business and getting Finkles off the market?

I thought it over even *more*. If I *tried* to make the shot and missed it, all I would get would be a bunch of stupid

Finkles to remind me of it for the rest of my life. And I couldn't even eat them, knowing they're filled with dangerous chemicals.

This was very puzzling!

I couldn't sleep. I got out of bed and went to look for Mom. She was reading the help wanted ads on a lawn chair in front of the trailer.

"You okay, Eddie?" she asked as I sat on her lap.

"I can't sleep."

"You've been quiet as a mouse all day," she said. "Something must be on your mind."

I had promised Mr. Finkle I wouldn't mention our conversation to anybody. But it didn't feel right keeping something this important from my mom. I needed advice. My mom was my mom and George Finkle was just a stranger. I decided to break the promise and tell Mom about Finkle's offer to give her back her job if I missed the shot.

It may have been puzzling to me, but it only took Mom about a second to make up *her* mind.

"Finkle must be pretty scared of you," Mom said softly. "I'm not going to tell you what to do, Eddie. But I know what I would do if I were in your position."

"What, Mom?"

"Go for the shot."

A Show of Appreciation

"Have you thought about our little chat, Eddie?" Finkle asked as soon as he recognized my voice on the phone.

"Yes. I've decided—"

"Before you tell me your decision, there was one more thing I wanted to throw at you, Eddie. Your mother said she was saving money to send you to college when you're older."

"Yeah?"

"Well, if you miss the shot on purpose, Eddie, I will pay all your expenses to put you through the college of your choice. What do you think of that?"

I didn't know *what* to think. He was trying to make me an offer I couldn't refuse. Maybe if I held out a while longer, he would throw in some cash, too. One thing was sure—Finkle *really* didn't want me to make the shot.

"Eddie, are you still on the line?"

"This is a bribe, isn't it?" I finally said. "You're trying to bribe me to miss the shot so you won't have to pay me a million dollars."

"Bribe is such an ugly word, Eddie. I'm simply offering you a college scholarship to show my appreciation. It's the least I can do after firing your mother."

"Mr. Finkle," I said, trying my best to sound assertive. "I've decided that I'm going to try to make the shot."

There was silence.

"Mr. Finkle, are you still on the line?"

"Okay, that's your decision," he said icily. "Good luck. You're going to need it."

"Uh, Mr. Finkle," I said. "One more thing. If I try to make the shot and miss it, does my mom *still* get her job back?"

He slammed down the phone without answering.

It seemed pretty clear that Finkle's offer was off the table now. Mom wouldn't get her job back no matter *what* I did. I would either win a million dollars, or I'd get nothing.

The Mystery Friend

AS SOON AS I TURNED down George Finkle's offer, strange things started happening. The phone rang one morning while Mom was out on a job interview. I picked it up.

"You're gonna miss, loser!" an eerie voice said.

"Who is this?" I demanded. But the caller hung up.

Early one morning, Annie knocked on the door and told me she wanted to show me something. She led me to a big patch of grass on a hill at the front of the trailer park.

Somebody had taken a lawnmower and mowed the words CHOKE ARTIST LIVES HERE into the grass.

The next day, when Annie and I went out to our old backboard to shoot a few foul shots, we saw from a distance that somebody had spray painted grafitti on the backboard. When we got closer we could see the words

E'ER BALL!

That kind of shook me, but I decided to stick around and shoot some foul shots anyway. I missed my first five in a row. That was unusual. I had practiced so much in the past month, I could practically sink foul shots in my sleep. But I just didn't seem to have the touch.

I tried some more, but I kept missing just about every shot. I had no idea what was wrong.

Finally, Annie shimmied up the pole to check the backboard. She was up there for a few minutes before she realized what the problem was.

"Hey!" she called down. "Somebody raised the rim!"

Sure enough, there were two lines on the pole where the backboard used to be bolted. The entire board had been raised a few inches. Somebody had gone through a lot of trouble to throw off my aim a little bit.

While all this was happening, every couple of days a strange letter would arrive in the mailbox. There was never a return address. This is what one of them said:

Dear MISSter Eddie Ball,

    Make no MISStake. You're going to MISS. I'm going to MISS you after you MISS. Will you MISS me?

       Your MISStery friend

Something told me that George Finkle's fat finger was involved in all these pranks. He was the one who would benefit the most if I missed the shot. And when I turned down his bribe, he sounded like he was out to get me.

"I ought to report Finkle to the FBI or the NBA or somebody," I told Annie after showing her the letter.

"I have a better idea," Annie said. "Keep your mouth shut. If word gets out that Finkle is trying to tamper with his own contest, the whole thing might be called off. And that's exactly what he wants."

"But I want to make him *pay* for this," I said, ripping up the letter.

"You want to make him pay?" Annie asked. "Make the shot."

She was right, of course. The more Finkle bothered me, I decided, the more determined I would become. Naturally, I wanted to sink the shot to get the million dollars. But I also wanted to sink the shot to drive George Finkle out of business.

One more strange thing happened in the middle of all this. I was practicing with Annie and her dad at the gym one afternoon, and the school band was rehearsing in there, too. It was hard to concentrate with all that noise. I was missing more shots than I usually do and Mr. Stokely pulled me aside.

"You know what an Achilles heel is, Eddie?"

"Some kind of shoe?" I guessed.

Annie thought that was funny, but her dad hushed her. "An Achilles heel is a weakness, and you've got one."

I knew very well what my weakness was. "Distraction," I said.

"That's right," Mr. Stokely agreed. "When it's just me and you in this gym, I've seen you hit 90, sometimes 95 percent of your shots. But as soon as there's some noise, a little commotion, you start to miss. Don't matter how good a shooter you are if you can't do it with the pressure on. And Madison Square Garden is gonna be *rockin'* when you step up to the foul line. It's gonna make *this* place sound like a tomb."

"I know."

"So what are you gonna do about it?"

"Concentrate harder," I said.

"No," Mr. Stokely corrected. "Concentrate less. Remember the abbreviation for mountain?"

"MT."

"Right. Empty your brain. Clean it out. Think of nothing. Now go back and try a few more."

I stepped up to the foul line and made a real effort to empty my brain. Just as I was about to release the first shot, Annie leaped in front of me.

"Ayeeeeeeeeeeeeeeee!" she screamed.

My shot missed. I set up to shoot another one and Mr. Stokely blew his whistle behind my head as I was about to shoot. The ball bounced off the rim.

"You're gonna have to work more on this," Mr. Stokely said.

At that moment, another noisy distraction caught my attention. At the far end of the gym, a guy fell off the bleachers. He hit the hardwood floor pretty hard and a camcorder slipped from his hand. He looked like the guy I'd spotted with the camcorder earlier, but I couldn't tell for sure. The guy struggled to his feet and quickly hobbled out of the gym without saying a word to anyone.

Now I was sure Finkle was spying on me.

12

Fame, Fortune, and Finkle

As THE NBA FINALS got closer, reporters from all over started calling. "Are you nervous?" they all wanted to know. "What will you do with the million dollars? What do you eat for breakfast?" and other silly stuff.

It was kind of cool in the beginning, being famous and all that. But after a while it got to be a drag. I'd be rushing out to practice and some guy would stick a microphone in my face and start asking questions. Reporters started following Mom around—even into the bathroom in a store—and she lost her patience. I tried to be as polite as I could.

A week before the NBA Finals, this article appeared in *USA Today*:

Shot of a lifetime

JACKSON, La.—How would you like to earn a million dollars for one second of work?

A Louisiana boy will have that opportunity on Saturday night. Eleven-year-old Eddie Ball won a poetry contest sponsored by Finkle Foods. Eddie will go to the charity stripe during halftime of Game 1 of the NBA Finals. He will have one shot. If he makes it, the youngster will go home with a check for one million dollars.

"Home" for the boy is on four wheels. Eddie lives in a trailer park with his mother, Rebecca Ball, an unemployed machine operator. Mrs. Ball, ironically, is a former employee of Finkle Foods. She was laid off recently.

How delicious it would be for young Eddie to become a millionaire at the expense of the company that fired his mother!

"Eddie's gonna make it," his mother told *USA Today.* "You can take it to the bank."

Eddie will have some help taking it to the bank. In his left back pocket, he carries a Susan B. Anthony silver dollar. He says it was given to him by his father, who passed away two years ago after contracting cancer.

Good luck charm or not, the word on the street is that this kid is shooting five hundred foul shots a day and making nine out of every ten. That would place him among the top free-throw shooters in the NBA this season.

The question is, can Eddie hit one out of one with the whole world watching him on Saturday?

By Rob Gleason, USA Today

13

What If I Miss?

THE LOS ANGELES LAKERS and New York Knicks each had a great season and rolled over their opponents in the playoffs. The two teams were scheduled to meet in the NBA Finals, which would start in Madison Square Garden.

In the days leading up to the Finals, I noticed that kids at school were acting differently around me. I wasn't used to so much attention. Everybody knew my name. One day I arrived at school and there was a big banner up over the front of the building—SINK IT, EDDIE! Some kids asked me for autographs. I didn't want to turn anybody down and act like a jerk. But I didn't want to pretend to be a celebrity and act like a jerk, either.

After phys ed one day, I was alone in the locker room when Ty and Johnny walked up to me. I was afraid they were going to beat me up, or worse. Instead, Ty stuck out his hand for me to shake.

"We want to apologize," he said.

"What for?"

"We were the ones who spray painted the backboard," Johnny admitted.

"And we mowed the grass, too," Ty said.

I looked at Ty, then at Johnny. Neither of them would meet my eye.

"You wrote the letters, too?" I asked.

"Yeah," Ty said, so softly I could barely hear.

"Which one of you came up with that brilliant idea?" I asked.

"A guy paid us," Johnny said, pulling a ten-dollar bill from his jeans.

"What guy?" I asked. "Finkle?"

"No, not Finkle," said Johnny. "I forget the guy's name."

"Try to remember!" I pleaded.

"It was one of those names that's spelled the same way forward and backward," Ty recalled. "You know, a . . . palindrome."

"Otto!" I exclaimed.

"Yeah, that's it."

"He's Finkle's flunkie," I told them.

"We're sorry, Eddie," Johnny said. "I guess we were jealous that you won the contest."

"So why are you telling me now?" I asked.

"Finkle fired a dozen more people," Ty said.

"Including our dads," added Johnny. "We want you to nail him."

"Nail him?" I asked. "What can I do?"

"Sink the shot, man," Ty said. "That's all. Sink the shot."

"I'm gonna try."

"One more thing, Eddie," Johnny said, holding out the ten-dollar bill. "You should have it."

"Keep the money," I said. "I'm gonna make Finkle pay me, too."

According to the rules of the contest, Finkle Foods had to pay to send the winner and his family to New York. I invited Annie and her dad to join Mom and me. We had become almost like a big family since the contest began.

I was nervous about the trip to New York. I had never been on a plane or visited a big city. At my last practice before the trip, I only sank seventy-one out of one hundred free throws. Good, but not great.

School let out for the summer on June 10. We were scheduled to fly out of Baton Rouge, Louisiana, on the twelfth, spend the next day in New York, and Game 1 would be on Saturday night, the fourteenth.

When I went to sleep the night before the trip, Mom came over to my bed to tuck me in. She and I had talked a lot about the million dollar shot. But we hadn't talked at all about what would happen afterward.

"Mom," I said, "if I make the shot, we're gonna move out of here."

"Oh yeah?"

"Yeah. We're gonna get a mansion somewhere. With a limo. And a pool. And helicopters and stuff."

"We don't need those things, Eddie."

"I'm gonna get it for you anyway." I sighed. "It's gonna be great."

"Sleep now," she whispered, kissing my forehead. "And dream of good things."

"Mom," I asked as she was getting up to leave, "what if I miss?"

"You won't," she said, stroking my head.

"But what if I do?" I asked. "Are you going to be mad at me?"

"Mad?" She looked surprised. "How could I be

mad at you for missing a foul shot?"

She ran her fingers through my hair the way she used to when I was little.

"The only thing that makes me mad and sad," she said, "is that your father won't be there to see you make the shot. He would have been so proud of you."

Memories of my dad were starting to slip away from me. It was getting harder to remember what he looked like. But I'll always remember the first time he took me out to shoot hoops. I must have been five or six. The ball felt like a boulder to me then. I kept shooting it with all my might and barely getting it over my own head. Each time, Dad caught the ball in the air, flipped it up into the basket, and told me I had gotten it in by myself.

"Nothin' but net!" he would shout, loud enough for the whole neighborhood to hear.

"Nothin' but net, Eddie," Mom whispered, flipping off the light.

"Nothin' but net, Mom."

14

The Million Dollar Shot

To GET OVER THE nervousness of my first plane ride, I got real goofy and obnoxious. There was a barf bag in the seat pocket in front of me, so I poked holes in it with a pen, put my fingers through them, and turned the bag into a puppet. I drew the face of a superhero on the front, a guy I called Vomit Man. Instead of fighting bad guys, he simply throws up on them.

Annie told me I was disgusting. My mom and Annie's dad, who were sitting behind us, just laughed.

When we lifted off the runway, my ears really started to hurt. Mom told me that was normal. I felt better after she gave me a stick of gum to chew. When the plane leveled off, the pilot's voice came over the loudspeaker.

"It has been brought to my attention," he said, "that we have a celebrity on our flight today."

Annie and I got up in our seats and looked around to see who it was. Neither of us had ever seen a real celebrity in person.

"It's Eddie Ball!" the pilot said. "He's the young man who will be shooting the million dollar foul shot during half-time of Game 1 at the NBA Finals in Madison Square Garden on Saturday night. Good luck, Eddie! You can do it!"

The whole cabin broke into applause, and Mom messed up my hair with her hand.

New York City was awesome! They put us up at this fancy hotel near Times Square, where they drop the ball on New Year's Eve. The Stokelys got one room and we got another. Each hotel room was bigger than our entire trailer! Annie came into our room and we jumped from bed to bed like a couple of lunatics.

The hotel had these really cool elevators that sort of hang on the side of the building, with the whole car exposed. Annie and I got into separate elevators and raced each other up to the forty-ninth floor and then back down to street level. It was a blast.

I was hoping that we would get to see the Empire State Building while we were in New York. Unfortunately, Annie's dad nixed that idea.

"If I know George Finkle," Mr. Stokely said, "he'll have you thrown *off* the Empire State Building to prevent you from taking the shot."

"Oh, come on, Dad!" laughed Annie.

"I *mean* it," Mr. Stokely said. "The man is evil."

Instead of sightseeing, the four of us spent the whole day in a ballroom at the hotel. The manager brought in a regulation basketball backboard and hoop for me. Mr. Stokely put me to work sinking foul shots.

I sank seventy-nine out of a hundred after breakfast, and he told me I could do better. In the afternoon I improved to eighty-five out of a hundred, but Mr. Stokely still wasn't satisfied.

"The basket is twice the diameter of the ball," he kept saying. "You've got no reason *ever* to miss."

The coolest part about the hotel was that we could just dial the front desk on the phone, order any food we wanted, and in a few minutes they'd bring it up to us. We didn't even have to pay for it because they just charged it to the room bill.

Annie and her dad came into our room and we ordered a big feast for dinner. We ate it while we watched TV. The news was all about murders and fires and other awful stuff. But then the sports guy came on and started talking about the NBA Finals and talking about *me.*

Too weird! Here I was a nobody from Louisiana eating room service in a fancy New York hotel while watching myself on TV. It was like *The Twilight Zone* or something.

"We tried to get an interview with young Eddie Ball," the sports guy said. "But he's in seclusion somewhere in a New York hotel tonight. Tomorrow at this time, he might be a millionaire. If you're listening, Eddie, knock 'em dead, kid! New York City is rootin' for ya!"

The game was scheduled for 7:30 P.M., which left the whole day for more practice. I sank 270 out of 300 in the morning and 92 out of 100 after lunch. Our folks were wandering around the hotel somewhere and I was halfway through my last hundred shots when Annie started waving her hands around like crazy.

"Eddie," she whispered. "C'mere!"

"What is it?"

"Shhhh! C'mere!"

The ballroom was divided in half by a large curtain. Annie was crouched at the side of the curtain, peeking through it.

"Your mom and my dad are *kissing*!" she said excitedly.

"Get out!"

I rushed over and tiptoed to where Annie was crouching. I poked my head through the curtain and there they were, Mom and Mr. Stokely, wrapped around each other like a couple of tangled-up vines.

I felt a sudden tightness in my shoulders. It felt like I had done a hundred pushups the day before. There was a pounding in my head, too.

"Ugh," I whispered. "I think I'm gonna throw up."

"*Grow* up, Eddie. In a couple of years all you'll want to do is kiss girls."

"No way."

"You will, too."

"Will not."

My first reaction to seeing my mom kissing Mr. Stokely was anger. I mean, after my dad died, in my head I knew and even hoped Mom would meet another man someday. And I knew Mr. Stokely was a great guy. But now that they were actually together, I was furious. Who said he could kiss my mom? Who said anybody could? Where they going to get married now? Did this make him my dad? I didn't like it one bit.

In the meantime, I had another problem on my hands. Crouching there next to each other, Annie's face was very close to mine. She kind of half closed her eyes, as if she was sleepy or something, and tilted her head a little to one side. I'd seen ladies do this in the movies just before they got kissed.

Did Annie want me to kiss her? Or maybe she just had a crick in her neck. Man, I wasn't sure I wanted to find out.

"I gotta practice," I muttered, and ran back to finish my last hundred shots.

Toward the end of practice, Mom and Mr. Stokely came out from behind the curtain, acting as if nothing unusual had been going on. I missed my next shot, and the two after that. I was seething.

"Whoa!" Mr. Stokely said, alarmed. "What's the matter, Eddie? I've *never* seen you miss three in a row."

"I've never seen you make out with my mom," I snapped as I missed another shot. *"That's* what's the matter."

Mom looked at Mr. Stokely. Mr. Stokely looked at Annie. Then everybody looked at me.

"I'm sorry I made you mad, Eddie," Mom said, putting her arm around me.

"But you're not sorry you did it."

"No, I'm not."

"How do you think Dad would feel?" I asked.

"I don't know," she replied. "I hope he would be happy that after he was gone I might be able to find someone else I want to be with. If I had gotten sick, I know I would have hoped he'd find someone after I was gone. Mr. Stokely is a good man, Eddie."

"Eddie," Mr. Stokely said softly. "My parents got divorced when I was a boy. Then one day my mom brought somebody else home. And I *hated* him! I called him names behind his back. In *front* of his back even. What right did *he* have to be hangin' around, watching our TV and eating our food? He wasn't my dad. But as time went by I could see that he and my mom really loved each other. They got married, too. It took a few years, but I stopped being mad at him. He'll never replace my dad, but he's my stepfather and we get along great now. I'm really glad my mom met him. So I know you're really angry right now, Eddie. But as time goes by, and if your mom and I get along, I hope maybe you won't be so angry at me. Think you might be able to give me a chance, Eddie?"

"Maybe," I sniffed.

"I'll accept that," he said. "But now I need to talk to

you, not as a man, not as a friend, and not as your mom's
boyfriend. I need to talk to you as your coach. In a little
while you're gonna take that shot. Distraction has always
been your biggest problem as a shooter, and right now
you're distracted by what you saw behind that curtain. You
have enough to worry about without worrying about me
and your mom. Tomorrow you can punch me, kick me,
and call me names. But tonight you gotta put that anger
out of your mind. Think you can do that?"

"I'll try," I said softly.

"You remember the abbreviation for mountain?"

"MT," I said.

"Right. Your mind should be totally empty. Now let's
finish up those last shots and do what we came here to
do."

I was still mad. But I had to admit he was right. Being
mad wasn't going to help me make the shot. It was just
another distraction and I had to put it out my mind like
any other distraction.

I went back to the line and found my groove again. My
499th shot of the day swished through the net. Number
500 bounced off the back rim. Mr. Stokely retrieved the
ball and told me to shoot one more.

"Never finish practice with a miss," he said. "You

need to walk out of here with confidence. And remember to bend your knees."

I swished the extra shot, and we gathered up our stuff to head for Madison Square Garden.

"This is it," Mr. Stokely said, burning his eyes into mine. "You ready?"

"Yeah."

"You feel good?"

"Yeah."

"You nervous?"

"No."

"You lyin'?"

"Yes."

"You gonna sink it anyway?"

"Yeah."

"I can't *hear* you!"

"I'm gonna sink it!" I shouted.

"Well, all right then, let's *do* it!"

Mr. Stokely knew his way around New York City because he had played college ball there. Walking down the street was weird. The first thing I noticed was that there was no grass. These puny trees were growing right out of little patches of dirt in the middle of concrete. Pigeons were all over the place, and they didn't even seem afraid of people. They'd fly right past your face. Actually, I was a little afraid of *them*.

And there were so many people! There would be like a hundred of them standing at a corner waiting for the light to change so they could cross the street. Back home, you'd only see that many people at a town meeting or something.

Some of the people on the street looked at me and nodded their head or gave me the thumbs up sign. I guess they recognized me from pictures in newspapers and magazines.

"Sink it, kid," an old lady said to me, slapping me five as she passed.

Everybody walked really fast. Some of them were talking on telephones. Annie told me to switch my good luck charm to my front pocket, because in New York pickpockets steal stuff from your back pockets and you never even feel a thing.

Mr. Stokely led us to Madison Square Garden, which was *really* awesome. When we told the security guards at the gate who I was and flashed them our passes, they ushered us inside like we were famous.

They took us right into the Knicks' locker room, which was really cool. I'd seen these guys on TV before, but meeting them in person was the best. Michael

Robinson! Juke Masters! Muhammed Aleem! I thought Mr. Stokely was a big guy, but some of these guys made him look *short.*

They all gathered around to shake my hand and wish me luck. Juke, who plays center for the Knicks, was putting on his sneakers. I guess he saw Annie and me staring at them. How could we help it? Each sneaker was about the size of a small boat.

"Go ahead," Juke said, "try 'em on."

Annie and I were able to put both our feet inside *one* of Juke's sneakers, and there was plenty of room left over.

"Hey, Mr. Millionaire, how about loanin' me a few thousand bucks?" Juke said, laughing.

"What if I miss the shot?" I asked.

"Get that word out of your vocabulary, kid," he said. "A fifteen-foot shot. Ten feet up. Nobody guarding you. No *problemo.* You can do it. You just have to forget about the crowd and cameras. Block 'em out. That's what I do."

I asked Juke for his autograph, and he asked me for mine, too. He said that once I became a millionaire, I would be famous just like him.

"Hey, kid," Juke asked, "how about you and your

girlfriend here join us in the shootaround?"

"I'm not his girlfriend," Annie said quickly. "What's a shootaround?"

"That's when we go out on the court before the game and . . . shoot around," Juke said.

We were excited to do it, but suddenly I sensed somebody was behind me. I turned around. It was George Finkle. He had appeared, like one of those vampires in the movies who swoops in out of nowhere.

"Eddie! I'm so happy to see you again!" he said in his slimy, insincere way. "I'd like you come with me to pose for pictures with some fans."

Annie looked at me and smirked. We both knew that Finkle didn't want me to have a chance to warm up before my million dollar shot.

"I may not get a chance to wish you good luck," Annie said before Finkle led me away. "You don't need it. You're the man."

Mr. Stokely gave me one last piece of advice. "The inflation hole," he said. "Focus on the inflation hole."

"Nothin' but net, Eddie," Mom whispered in my ear. "Nothin' but net."

Finkle escorted me out of the locker room. In the hallway there were a few hundred fans waiting. Each of them was holding a large piece of cardboard with the words SINK IT, ED! printed on it.

They gathered around me, clapping me on the back and kissing me and stuff. Boy, and they say people in New York aren't friendly! These people were all *over* me. Some of them just wanted to touch my clothes, like I was a celebrity.

A photographer got them all to hold up their signs and pose around me.

"Closer to Eddie!" the photographer shouted as they crushed around me. "Closer!"

When the photographer was done, Finkle led me to his private box high up in the Garden. There was a fat lady and a fat kid sitting there. Finkle's family, undoubtedly. I wanted to watch the first half of the game with Mom and Annie and her dad, but Mr. Finkle said the crowd might start a riot if they saw me before halftime. Mom and my friends would have courtside seats, he assured me.

There were all kinds of food and stuff in the private box. They even had waiters *bring* it to you. So this is how rich people live, I thought. I could get used to it.

"How do you feel, Eddie?" Finkle asked. He was eating a pork chop, the juice dribbling down his chin.

"Like a million bucks," I replied. Finkle started to choke on the pork chop. I thought I might have to perform the

Heimlich maneuver on him, but his son smacked him on the back and he stopped gagging. The kid must have been about six or seven and looked like Dennis the Menace.

"My daddy told me we're rich and you're poor," the kid said. "But if you make the shot, we'll be poor and you'll be rich. So I hope you miss."

"Thanks for the pep talk," I told him.

The Lakers had a five-point lead after the first quarter, but I was too nervous to pay much attention to the game. All I could think about was my shot. I paced around the room, trying to form an image in my head of the ball dropping through the net. Finkle had a waiter get me a soda. He also brought a big plate of shrimp, which I love but hardly ever get to eat because it's real expensive. I wolfed down a bunch of them.

With just a few minutes left in the first half, Finkle suggested I put on my Finkle sweatshirt and head down toward the court with him.

In the elevator, I began feeling a little light-headed. I haven't been in many elevators, and I thought that was why I was feeling weird. But it hadn't bothered me when Annie and I were racing the elevators back at the hotel. I figured it was just stage fright. Or who knows, maybe I ate too many shrimp?

"Isn't it thrilling, Eddie?" Finkle asked. "You know, this game is being broadcast globally by satellite. People will be watching you from all around the world. This could be the most widely watched television event since J. R. was shot."

I didn't know who J. R. was, and I didn't care. Walking through the tunnel that led to the court, I was starting to feel like somebody had shot *me*. I was sweating and I felt a little dizzy.

By the time we got to the side of the court, it was half-time and I felt really sick. I glanced at the scoreboard. The Knicks were up by two points. The court was cleared.

Finkle led me out to the foul line with his arm around my shoulders. A buzz started building in the crowd. I was feeling nervous and jumpy, but nothing was going to stop me from taking this shot.

"Ladies and gentlemen," boomed the public address announcer, *"if you direct your attention to the foul line on the east side of the court, we would like to introduce eleven-year-old Eddie Ball, winner of the Finkle Million Dollar Shot Contest. It was Eddie who asked the question: 'How could the Pilgrims e'er be contented, / When savory Finkles had not been invented?'"*

The crowd erupted into cheers. There was a smattering of hoots, too. I thought I heard some people chanting "Air Ball! Air Ball!"

When Finkle and I reached the foul line, I looked around and spotted Annie, Mom, and Mr. Stokely at courtside. They waved and gave me the thumbs up sign. Behind the backboard, a bunch of those fans I posed with were holding up their SINK IT, ED! signs.

There was one of those huge DiamondVision screens in the corner of the Garden. They usually use it to show instant replays and commercials. Right now, the camera was trained on my face.

It's pretty weird seeing your head blown up to the size of a truck. I raised my eyebrow and watched the enormous eyebrow shoot up on the screen at the exact same instant. I touched my nose and this gigantic finger touched the nose on the screen. It felt like I was playing one of those virtual reality video games. It was disorienting.

"*Ladies and gentlemen,*" the PA announcer continued, "*if Eddie can make this shot, he will be one million dollars richer.*"

The crowd started cheering and stamping their feet. Finkle leaned over to me. "I'll give you one last chance to accept my offer, Eddie. Tell me you'll miss right now. Your mom gets her job back, and you get a free ride to the college of your choice. Think about it, Eddie."

"I thought about it," I said without hesitation. "I didn't come this far to take a dive."

"Suit yourself, Eddie."

As the referee handed me the ball, Finkle waved to the fans sitting behind the basket. Suddenly, as a group, they turned around all their SINK IT, ED! signs. On the back of each one was a large photo of a basketball backboard that looked exactly like the backboard at the Garden.

So instead of just *one* backboard to aim for, there was an ocean of hundreds of them in front of me. It was like I was looking through a kaleidoscope.

"You are a . . ." I struggled to find the right word to describe George Finkle. "Fink," I finally said.

"Business is business," Finkle replied. "That's what your mom said. You gotta do what you gotta do."

"After I sink this shot, you're going *out* of business," I told him as I bounced the ball three times on the foul line. "Better get out your checkbook."

"I don't think that will be necessary, Eddie," he chuckled. "There's no way you're going to make this shot. Look at you. You're so nervous you're shaking. The whole world is going to watch you fail, Eddie. Then you'll go home and all the kids at school are going to make fun of you. For the rest of your life you'll be thinking how things would have turned out differently if you had only made this shot."

"Say whatever you want," I barked at him. "I'm still going to make the shot."

"You sound pretty confident, Eddie," he said. "I guess it's because of your lucky silver dollar, huh?"

I patted the pocket where I'd put my Susan B. Anthony. There was no bump. I reached inside the pocket. My lucky silver dollar wasn't there.

"Something wrong, Eddie?" Finkle asked innocently. "You look a little pale."

My shirt was drenched with sweat. The crowd was screaming and pounding the floor with their feet thunderously. Some of the Knicks and Lakers had filed out of the locker room and gathered at the edge of the court to watch. I could feel my heart beating in my chest. I felt like I might faint.

Mom rushed over from her seat at the side of the court.

"What's wrong, Eddie?" she asked.

"I can't do it," I said. "My Susan B. Anthony dollar is gone! Somebody took it. Probably while I was posing for pictures before."

"Susan B. Anthony can't shoot 90 percent from the line," Mom said. *"You* can, Eddie!"

The crowd was getting restless. They didn't know what was going on and they were impatient for me to take my shot so the second half of the game could begin.

"What seems to be the problem, Eddie?" Finkle asked with this sweet smile that made me want to punch his lights out. "Do you want some more shrimp? How about a Finkle?" He pulled one out of his pocket.

"Mom, I've got triple vision," I said, holding her arm for support. "I see three rims out there."

"Well," chortled Finkle, "just aim for the one in the middle, Eddie!"

"You better shut up, fat boy!" Mom said, grabbing Finkle by the lapels of his suit, "and let my son take his shot."

Finkle stumbled back to the top of the key, stunned. I stepped to the line again and bounced the ball three times. The noise level in the Garden was building, like a drumroll. I peered at the rim. I couldn't focus my eyes. I tried to focus on the inflation hole, but that didn't work, either.

I stepped back off the line again and scanned the edge of the court for Annie. I caught her eye and motioned her to come over. Some of the crowd cheered as she dashed across the court.

"What is it, Eddie?" she asked. "Are you okay?"

"I can't do it," I said. "I can't block out the distractions. I think I might pass out. You gotta take the shot for me."

"Are you crazy? I'm not putting on a sweatshirt that says Finkle on it. I can't represent that slave driver—"

"Forget about that stuff for once!" I begged her, holding out the ball. "I *need* you. You know you can sink it. And after all, you wrote the stupid poem to begin with. Please . . ."

She looked at me for a moment. Then she reached out and took the ball from me.

"Okay," Annie said. "I'll do it."

The crowd went crazy. Annie stepped to the line, bounced the ball slowly three times, and glanced at the basket.

"Wait just a minute!"

It was George Finkle. He snatched the ball from Annie's hands.

"I'm sorry you've got the jitters, Eddie, but the rules of the contest indicate quite clearly that there can be no substitutions. It was your name on the entry form, Eddie, and you've got to take the shot yourself. I'm afraid I'll have to ask you to go back to your seat, young lady."

"MT, Eddie!" Annie said. "Get your head empty!"

The crowd booed when Annie gave him the ball and walked slowly back to her seat. Finkle waited until everybody had settled down before handing me the ball.

I looked up at the rim again. I squared my feet to the line and bounced the ball three times.

"Do it, Eddie," Mom said.

I scanned the seats one more time for Annie. When she caught my eye, she looked at me and deliberately closed her eyes.

I looked at her quizzically. She stared right back. She put her fingers up to her eyelids and pretended she was pulling her eyelids down like they were window shades.

No, I thought to myself, shaking my head. She's crazy. She's out of her mind. I can't take the most important shot of my life with my eyes closed!

"Take the shot already!" somebody shouted from the crowd.

I looked toward Annie again. She was smiling at me and nodding insistently. She closed her eyes again.

I looked at the rim. It appeared to be moving backward and forward. I couldn't judge the distance anymore.

I didn't know how hard to shoot the ball.

I closed my eyes. The entire crowd must have been watching me on the DiamondVision screen, because everyone gasped at once. Madison Square Garden was filled with 20,000 people, but suddenly they were totally silent.

With my eyes closed, a lot of the distractions disappeared. I didn't see all those cardboard backboards Finkle had given out. I didn't see the thousands of people staring at me. I didn't see the DiamondVision screen.

I didn't see the rim, either. But it was okay. In the thousands of foul shots I had taken while practicing for this moment, my mind had *learned* where the rim was. The muscles in my legs knew how much to bend my knees. The muscles in my arms knew where to aim the ball, how high to arc it.

I took a deep breath. I raised the ball up. I bent my knees.

I shot.

15

Slow-Mo

Unconsciously or not, I gave the ball a little extra push. If I missed, I wanted to miss long. At least there was the chance the ball would bounce off the backboard and drop in. No way I was going to chuck an air ball.

As soon as I released the ball, I opened my eyes. I could see it as if it was in slow motion, rotating backward.

The ball was just a little high and slightly left of where I wanted it to be. It hit the backboard and bounced down. It struck the left side of the rim and rolled forward on it.

The ball tipped over toward the middle of the rim slightly, which gave it a little speed. It continued rolling around the front of the rim, going counterclockwise until it reached the back. It kept right on rolling around the rim two more revolutions, as if it was caught in a whirlpool.

The ball was losing speed now. It was just a question

of whether it would topple over on the inside of the rim
and into the net or outside the rim.

"Roll *in*!" Mom screamed.

"Roll *out*!" screamed George Finkle.

All anybody could do was watch and wait.

16

The End?

THERE ARE A FEW ways this story could end:

1. I could have missed the shot. If that happened, you'd probably be real disappointed. Most people don't like unhappy endings.

2. I could have made the shot. If that happened, you might also be disappointed. A lot of people would say that ending was predictable. They'd say they knew all along I would make the shot. And so many stories have these happy, sappy endings.

3. The story could end right *here*, leaving you guessing about whether or not the ball went in the net. If that happened, you'd probably be *really* disappointed. Maybe even angry. Who wants to read

a whole book and have it end with the ball hanging in midair?

I guess the best thing to do is just to tell you what actually
happened.

17

Okay, the Real Ending

So, AS I WAS SAYING, the ball was losing speed. It was just a matter of whether it would topple over on the inside of the rim and into the net or outside the rim. It was out of my hands. All I could do was watch and wait.

And then the ball dropped through the net.

Pandemonium. It was like fireworks went off inside Madison Square Garden.

"Yesssss!" Mom shouted, punching her fist in the air. She grabbed me and wrapped her arms around me like a boa constrictor. It was just as well, because I would have collapsed to the court otherwise.

I wasn't thinking about the million dollars. I wasn't thinking about the shot. I was just thinking it was over. I did what I went there to do, and it felt great.

Annie and her dad came running over and leaped on us. We were all crying and stuff, and I didn't even care if anybody saw it.

"You're the man with the plan!" Annie shouted. "The man with the plan!"

"It wasn't pretty." Mr. Stokely laughed. "But you'll take it, right?"

"I couldn't have done it without you guys," I said, and I meant it, too.

Meanwhile, George Finkle sat right down on the court with a thud and put his head in his hands. He was crying, too, but something told me they weren't tears of joy.

When Mom finally let me go, I tore off the Finkle sweatshirt like it was on fire and threw it into the crowd.

Some of the Knicks came out to half-court carrying a check that was about the size of a garage door. One line on the check said: PAY TO THE ORDER OF EDDIE BALL. The next line said: ONE MILLION DOLLARS AND 00/100 CENTS. And on the bottom was George Finkle's big, fat signature.

Juke Masters shook my hand and held the enormous check with me while a bunch of photographers took pictures. Juke towered over everybody and Annie cracked, "Hey, Juke, is that your *personal* check?"

"I don't know how we're going to get it through the door at home," Mom said.

"So have Eddie buy you a new house!" joked Juke.

As we walked off the court to the cheering of the crowd, I noticed George Finkle was still sitting right there on the court, bawling like a baby. I went over to him.

"Hey, Georgie," I said cheerfully. "Wanna go for double or nothing?"

"I don't have double," he sobbed. "I have nothing."

I actually felt a little sorry for him. *Very* little! I put my hand on his shoulder. "Mr. Finkle, I just wanted to let you know that if you need a place to live, I think our trailer may be available."

Well, what did you think? Like I was going to say something *nice* to that jerk?

Afterward . . .

The Knicks won, but we didn't stick around to watch the second half of the game. I needed some fresh air, so we left the Garden and walked down Thirty-Fourth Street.

"Look!" Annie shouted after we'd walked a bit. "The Empire State Building!"

We rushed inside, bought tickets, and rode the elevator up to the observation deck. It was a clear night. As we stepped out on the deck, we could see just about forever in every direction—the World Trade Center and the Statue of Liberty to the south, the George Washington Bridge and Central Park to the north. A cool wind blew through my hair, reviving me. New York City looked beautiful.

"I *told* you we'd be on top of the world someday," I said to Mom.

Annie and I poked our heads through the fence and peered down at the cars below. The world looked like a gigantic MicroMachines set.

"Hey, wanna see me spit?"

"Eddie, don't!" Annie yelled. "You could kill some-body!"

"Kill somebody with *spit*?"

"You know," Annie said, "now that you're a million-aire, people will expect you to act dignified."

"I thought the great thing about being rich was that nobody could tell you what to do."

Mom and Mr. Stokely said they were going to go around the other side of the observation deck and look at Brooklyn, where Mr. Stokely grew up. Annie and I stared off into the tip of Manhattan.

"How do you feel?" Annie asked.

"Like I'm in a dream," I said. "I keep thinkin' I'm gonna wake up and we'll be back home playing HORSE."

"I don't know if I can beat you anymore," she said. "Now that you know how to shoot with your eyes closed."

"You know, I said I'd give you half the money if I made the shot," I told Annie. "I meant it."

"Don't be crazy, Eddie. Buy something outrageous for yourself. The world is your oyster."

"I hate oysters."

"You know what I mean."

This was new to me. Mom and I had plenty of days when our problem was scraping together enough money to pay the bills. Now the problem was figuring out what I should do with the money I had.

"There's lots of cool stuff you can buy with a million dollars," Annie pointed out. "Your own basketball court . . ."

"A new car for my mom and your dad . . . ," I added.

"A house that doesn't have wheels under it . . ."

"Jobs for our folks."

"You can't buy a job," Annie said. "Besides, with a million bucks you don't need a job. You can buy a whole *company* and hire people to do the jobs for you."

Slowly, Annie and I turned toward each other. She had

a devilish gleam in her eye. I think it hit both of us at the exact same moment. There was one thing that would be the absolute coolest thing to buy in the whole world. We said it together—

"Finkle Foods!"

The day after I made the shot, the Food and Drug Administration announced that Finkles cause cancer. George Finkle shut down the Finkle Foods factory and put the company up for sale real cheap. Mom, Mr. Stokely, Annie, and I formed our own company and bought out Finkle.

I named Mom the company chef and put her in charge of dreaming up new snack foods. I figured Mr. Stokely would be great at helping everybody do their jobs better, and I gave him the title of chief operating officer. I put Annie in charge of writing all our advertising. And me, well, I didn't really know what my role in the company should be. So I had some business cards printed up that simply read:

Eddie Ball
Big Shot

Our first official act as a company was to rehire all the workers Finkle laid off. Next, we stopped production of Finkles and retooled the factory to make Air Crunchies, the low-fat cracker snack that Mom invented. Finally, we renamed Finkle Foods "The Air Ball Company."

And you know what our new slogan is?

How could the Pilgrims e'er be contented,
When Air Ball Crunchies had not been invented?

I kind of like the sound of that, don't you?

The Poetry Book Society
Anthology 1989–1990

The
Poetry Book Society
Anthology 1989–1990

Edited with an introduction by
CHRISTOPHER REID

Hutchinson
London Sydney Auckland Johannesburg

All rights reserved

This edition first published in 1989 by Hutchinson Ltd.,
an imprint of Century Hutchinson Ltd., Brookmount House,
62–65 Chandos Place, London WC2N 4NW,
and by the Poetry Book Society Ltd.,
21 Earls Court Square, London SW5

Century Hutchinson Australia (Pty) Ltd.,
20 Alfred Street, Milsons Point, Sydney 2016, Australia

Century Hutchinson New Zealand Ltd.,
PO Box 40–086, 32–34 View Road, Glenfield, Auckland 10

Century Hutchinson South Africa (Pty) Ltd.,
PO Box 337, Bergvlei 2012, South Africa

Phototypeset in Linotron Times
by Input Typesetting Ltd., London
Printed and bound in Great Britain by
Courier International, Tiptree, Essex

British Library Cataloguing in Publication Data

The Poetry Book Society anthology, 1989–1990.
  I. Reid, Christopher *1949–* II. Poetry Book Society
  821'.914

  ISBN 0–09–173992–6

Contents

Editor's Introduction ix
Simon Armitage   Eighties, Nineties   1
                      The Civilians   4
Connie Bensley   Caller   6
                      Bottleneck   7
Eavan Boland   The Achill Woman   8
Alan Brownjohn   Lucky Thirteen   10
Gillian Clarke   The Wind Park   11
David Constantine   Local Historian   12
Wendy Cope   Exchange of Letters   13
Robert Crawford   Harris   15
Neil Curry   Skulls   16
Helen Dunmore   Lutherans   18
Douglas Dunn   The Crossroads of the Birds 20
Alistair Elliot   A Relic   22
                      Learning to Swim   23
D. J. Enright   As You Say   24
                      Going Abroad?: a Leaflet   25
Gavin Ewart   Radio Cricket   26
                      Public Opinion   27
U. A. Fanthorpe   King Edward's Flora   28
Vicki Feaver   Anna the Javanese   30
Elaine Feinstein   Infidelities   31
Roy Fisher   Going   32
                      Hypnopaedia   33
John Fuller   In the Quarry   34
Roger Garfitt   Hares Boxing   35
James Greene   Minster Lovell   38
                      In a Church Tower (from the
                      German of Mörike)   39
Philip Gross   Snapshots of a Holiday   40
                      Away from It All   42

David Harsent	Childe	44
	Poem with Red Armchair	46
Seamus Heaney	*from* Lightenings	47
Selima Hill	A Small Hotel	52
Michael Hofmann	*Schönlaternengasse*	53
Alan Hollinghurst	Dry Season Nights	54
Ted Hughes	Mayday	55
Robert Johnstone	Murdering Democracy	57
John Levett	A Slip	58
Grevel Lindop	Games of Chance	59
Christopher Logue	Some Lines from *War Music 2*, an Account of Books 1–4 of Homer's *Iliad*	61
E. A. Markham	Nibble, Nibble	64
Harold Massingham	Tree-dream	65
Medbh McGuckian	Hessian, Linen, Silk	67
Ian McMillan	The Making of the English Working Class	68
Paul Muldoon	The Nest	69
Paul Munden	Hell Creek	70
	That's What This Is	72
Don Paterson	Perigee	74
Tom Paulin	*from* Seize the Fire	75
Peter Porter	At Schubert's Grave	77
Craig Raine	The Explorers	78
Tom Rawling	Gas Drill	82
Tom Raworth	*from* Eternal Sections	83
Peter Reading	Prouerbes xxij. iij	84
Peter Redgrove	Carcass and Balsam	85
Oliver Reynolds	Professor	86
Carol Rumens	Prelapsarian	87
Deirdre Shanahan	Under the Trees	88
Penelope Shuttle	Mademoiselle	89
Stephen Spender	Letter from Antarctica	90
Matthew Sweeney	The Dark	91

George Szirtes	Losing	92
Charles Tomlinson	The Blade	93
	Apples Painted	94
Martin Turner	Colonies	95
	The Porous Garden	97
Hugo Williams	Lost Lines	98
	Lunch Hour	99

EDITOR'S INTRODUCTION

Genesis, II, 19

with thanks to the poets

The Old Testament being wrong
in one detail

it was the animals came to Adam
and told him their names

different voices
and listening hard

he found he liked some
better than others

more melodious
howls and growls

more eloquent squawks
and so he asked them

would they stick around
and sing to him sometimes

by virtue the world's first
zoo-keeper and anthologist

SIMON ARMITAGE

Eighties, Nineties

Firstly, we worked in laughable conditions.
The photocopier
defied definition,
the windows were sealed with a decade of paintwork,
the thought of a cigarette triggered the sprinklers
and the security door
was open to question.
Any excuse got me out of the office.

I found the letter in the 'pending' folder,
a handwritten thing
signed T. Ruth O'Reilly
on a perfumed leaf of watermarked vellum.
It requested recognition, or maintenance even
from a putative father,
one William Creamstick
who was keeping shtum in the Scottish Borders.

At midnight I took the decision to risk it.
I darned the elbows
of my corduroy jacket,
threw a few things in an old army surplus
and thumbed it to Ringway for a stand-by ticket.
At dawn I was still
going round in circles
in a five-mile stack over Edinburgh airspace.

I accepted a lift to Princes Street Gardens
from an aftershave rep
who slipped me some samples.
It was Marie Celeste-ville in the shopping centre

so I borrowed a pinta from the library doorstep
and a packet of rusks
from the all-night chemist
then kipped for an hour in the cashpoint lobby.

Creamstick's house was just as I'd pictured:
pigs in the garden,
geese in the kitchen.
He was toasting his feet on the coal-fired Aga
as I rapped the window with my umbrella handle
and he beckoned me in,
thinking I'd come
to spay the bitches in his sheep-dog's litter.

He listened, nodding, as though I were recounting
the agreeable facts
from another man's story.
The producing a bread knife the size of a cutlass
he suggested, in short, that I vacate his premises
and keep my proboscis
out of his business
or he'd reacquaint me with this morning's breakfast.

In a private wood on the way to the trunk-road
I stumbled on a fish farm
and beyond its embankment
was a fish that had jumped too far from the water.
Two more minutes of this world would have killed it.
I carried it, drowned it,
backstroked its gills
till it came to its senses; disappeared downwards.

Back at Head Office they were all going apeshit.
Hadn't I heard of
timesheets, or clearance,

or codes of conduct, or agency agreements?
As I handed my keys in and typed out my notice
I left them with this
old tandem to ride on:
if you only pay peanuts, you're working with monkeys.

SIMON ARMITAGE

The Civilians

We signed the lease and knew we were landed.
Our dream house: half farm, half mansion; gardens
announcing every approach, a greenhouse
   with a southern aspect.
   Here the sunlight lasted;
evenings stretched their sunburnt arms towards us,
held us in their palms: gilded us, warmed us.

We studied the view as if we owned it;
noted each change, nodded and condoned it.
We rode with the roof down, and if the days
   overstepped themselves
   then the golden evenings
spread like ointment through the open valleys,
buttered one side of our spotless washing.

Forget the dangers of iron pyrites
or the boy who ran from his mother's farm
to the golden house on the other hill
   which was a pigsty
   taking the sunlight.
This was God's glory. The big wheel had stopped
with our chair rocking sweetly at the summit.

For what we have, or had, we are grateful.
   To say otherwise
   would be bitterness
and we know better than to surrender.
Behind the hen-house the jalopy is snookered:
   its bodywork sound,
   its engine buggered

but still there is gold: headlights on the road,
the unchewable crusts of our own loaves,
    old leaves the dog drags in.
    Frost is early this Autumn.
    Wrapped up like onions
we shuffle out over the frozen ground;
prop up the line where our sheets are flagging.

Caller

Why does she allow it?
She looks down with distaste
at his vulgar brown curls,
his red pointed tongue slipping in and out
over the blue vein in the curve
of her arm. The clock nags; the air
suffocates with carnations.

In the middle of a resolve
to run from the room, she leans back
to catch her breath, and slides her feet
out of her purple slippers.

His tongue begins to travel.

CONNIE BENSLEY

Bottleneck

The bottleneck
in her journey home that night
was the down escalator at Knightsbridge.

He chose to wait there,
looking upwards
for her clocked black stockings,
the red flared skirt,
the swinging plait.

When she saw him
she turned back in a flash
climbing, stumbling,
passing and re-passing
the bra-and-pantie girl
with her languorous glance
and her cleavage
           cleavage
           cleavage

EAVAN BOLAND

The Achill Woman

She came up the hill carrying water.
She wore a half-buttoned, wool cardigan,
a tea-towel round her waist.

She pushed the hair out of her eyes with
her free hand and put the bucket down.

The zinc-music of the handle on the rim
tuned the evening. An Easter moon rose.
In the next-door field a stream was
a fluid sunset; and then, stars.

I remember the cold rosiness of her hands.
She bent down and blew on them like broth.
And round her waist, on a white background,
in coarse, woven letters, the words 'glass cloth'.

And she was nearly finished for the day.
And I was all talk, raw from college –
week-ending at a friend's cottage
with one suitcase and the set text
of the Court poets of the Silver Age.

We stayed putting down time until
the evening turned cold without warning.
She said goodnight and started down the hill.

The grass changed from lavender to black.
The trees turned back to cold outlines.
You could taste frost

but nothing now can change the way I went
indoors, chilled by the wind
and made a fire
and took down my book
and opened it and failed to comprehend

the harmonies of servitude,
the grace music gives to flattery
and language borrows from ambition –

and how I fell asleep
oblivious to

the planets clouding over in the skies,
the slow decline of the Spring moon,
the songs crying out their ironies.

ALAN BROWNJOHN

Lucky Thirteen

Don't call, just come. Come into the room,
Hang your shirt over the mirror and 'feel free'.
I put the telephone down in that corner,
Underneath my nightdress. The air conditioning?
Noisy, probably safe; but I'll play some rock.
Sit down in one chair and hold conversation
To start. Any more, write it down, *write it down*!
. . . Prepare yourself to wake quickly if you sleep,
And I hope you not talk in your sleep.
From here you will see the sun rise over
The Heroes' Monument. If it does,
And you stay long enough for that, it will be
The first times we ever kiss in daylight.

GILLIAN CLARKE

The Wind Park

At first barely discernible,
a faint line drawn in graphite
on a water-marked page,
hairline crack in a bird's skull.

Then one evening to the west
where light dissolves in wind and water
another rises tall as sky
to finger prevailing westerlies.

When the swallows come home
they'll ride the tangled currents
through webs of steel where once
was a wide aisle of air.

First they raised stones.
cromlechs, megaliths, as step by step
from winter's narrowest day
they counted home the sun.

Now they hoist delicate masts,
a steel circle to crown a hill,
moth-blur of blades against the light,
generating fire out of air.

DAVID CONSTANTINE

Local Historian

Come in for a reference he lay down,
The book on his chest, his finger trapped in its pages.
Slept, and the sea did what it always does
When we sleep and listen, the sea drew nearer
And the neighbourly black cypresses
Almost leaned over the house. Starlings
Drove like hail to the collection in the marshes.

Slept, out of hours, late winter in the afternoon,
His finger marking a reference, and with a whisper,
A shush, an exhalation, his library
Dissolved and a thousand saints and the local worthies,
Every carn and cross and cove, as fine as flour,
Sucked from the room like dust, like spores,
Name after name after name, the parishes,

All of Cornwall, slipped from his lease
Towards home. When he wakes, in the darkness
For a while he will not know where he is,
The sea making a din, the cypresses overwhelming.
But I know that man. His finger marking the place
He will go back to the lighted room where his writing is,
He will recall the truant parishes, once more.

WENDY COPE

Exchange of Letters

Man who is a serious novel would like to hear from a woman who is a poem.' Classified advertisement, *New York Review of Books*

Dear Serious Novel,

I am a terse, assured lyric with impeccable rhythmic flow, some apt and original metaphors and a music that is all my own. Some people say I am beautiful.

My vital statistics are eighteen lines, divided into three-line stanzas, with an average of four words per line.

My first husband was a cheap romance; the second was *Wisden's Cricketers' Almanac*. Most of the men I meet nowadays are autobiographies, but a substantial minority are books about photography or trains.

I have always hoped for a relationship with an upmarket work of fiction. Please write and tell me more about yourself.

Yours intensely,

Song of the First Snowdrop

Dear Song of the First Snowdrop,

Many thanks for your letter. You sound like just the sort of poem I am hoping to find. I've always preferred short, lyrical women to the kind who go on for page after page.

I am an important 150,000 word comment on the dreams and dilemmas of twentieth century Man. It took six years to attain my present weight and stature but all the 27 publishers I have so far approached have failed to understand me. I have my share of sex and violence and a very good joke in chapter nine, but to no avail. I am sustained by the belief that I am ahead of my time.

Let's meet as soon as possible. I am longing for you to read me from cover to cover and get to know my every word.

Yours impatiently,

Death of the Zeitgeist

ROBERT CRAWFORD

Harris

So many days: a day to paint the oil storage tank;
A day to stocktake the shop's wooden shelves;
A day for blasting new road.

Now it's impossible to remember
What day their old Ford was pushed down the field
'Towards Canada' as the joke had it then,

Or just when that front door first
Missed out, and started to show
Its turquoise undercoat.

No one on the island would touch it up
Or unscrew below its missing panes
The white iron numeral 4.

NEIL CURRY

Skulls

For John Wood

Down where the swash and backwash of the tide
Had retched up wet entanglements
Of bladderwrack and kelp, the usual
Goitred orange and a single shoe,
We found the dead gannet;

Its intricate, slim wings intact as when
We saw them fold like paper darts
And plunge into the seas round Borreray;
And still with that slight blush of yellow
To the head, like a girl's chin

When you hold a buttercup beneath it.
And I wanted that skull – the great beak
Longer than my longest finger – to put
Beside the hooked and sun-bleached hawk's
On my windowsill.

But lifting it I found the tongue gone
And a thick gruel of maggots
Already on the boil in its gullet.
And I couldn't touch it. We walked off
Talking of flowers instead:

Of the misty and paler-than-harebell blue
Of sea holly, Crippen's henbane,
And the trumpets of sea convolvulus
Like the horns of ancient gramophones
Shaped out of porcelain.

But looking back I saw how the wind lifted
One wing and let if flap and fall
Like Ahab's arm when the white whale sounded,
Breached and rolled. And I thought of others
That I had missed out on:

Those oiled razorbills at St Bees,
The rat-gnawed heron on the banks
Of the Nene, and I knew that the only way
To win skulls such as those would have been
To take a knife to them,

Slicing into feather and skin, probing
For the vertebrae, to sever
Cartilage and ligament and cut through
To the bone. It's either that or waiting
For the sea's gift, or the sun's.

HELEN DUNMORE

Lutherans

Whichever way I turned on the radio
there was Sibelius
or an exceptionally long weather forecast.
Good practice: I'd purse up my lips
to the brief gulp of each phrase.

Sometimes I struck a chord with the World Service's
sense-fuzz, like the smell of gardenia
perfume in Woolworth's: instantly cloying,
the kind that doesn't bloom on your skin,

or, in the 2 pm gloom of the town square,
I'd catch the pale flap of a poster
for the *Helsingin Sanomat*: POMPIDOU KUOLLUT.
I'd buy one, but never wrestle beyond the headline.

When pupils asked what I thought of 'this three-day week'
I'd mention the candle-blaze
nightly in my room during the power cuts,
and the bronchitis I had,
but I'd balance the fact that I smoked too much
against the marsh-chill when the heating went off,
and weigh black cars loaded with ministers
against the altar-effect in my bedroom.

I'd always stop on the railway bridge
even at one in the morning. The city was shapeless,
        squeezed in
by hills bristling with Sitka spruce.
The drunks had their fires lit
but they were slow, vulnerable, frozen

while flaming on a half-litre from the State Alcohol Shop.

If their luck held they'd bunch on the Sports Hall heating
        grates
rather than be chipped free from a snow heap
in the first light of ten in the morning,
among a confusion of fur-hatted burghers
going to have coffee and cakes.
Work started at eight, there was never enough time.
They'd stop, chagrined, and murmur 'It's shocking'.

They were slowly learning not to buy the full-cream milk
of their farming childhoods; there was a government campaign
with leaflets on heart disease and exercise
and a broadsheet on the energy crisis
with diagrams suggesting the angle
beyond which windows should never be opened.

Their young might be trim, but they kept
a pious weakness for sinning on cake
and for those cloudy, strokeable hats
that frame Lutheran pallor.
After an evening visit to gym, they'd roll
the green cocoon of their ski-suited baby
onto the pupils' table. Steadied with one hand
it lay prone and was never unpacked.

DOUGLAS DUNN

The Crossroads of the Birds

High on the draining ridges, a road is blue
Reflected puddles for a laverock's
Mirrored lyric; and he is here, the true
Beggar, ancestral and unorthodox.

It is the time of the crucifix, old
Pre-Reformation days and a bad year
For war; the hairst is sour and thin, and its cold
Tenantry deaf to the stonechat and wheatear.

Men with steel hands are riding on this road.
He hears them miles away, then sniffs the rain
Approaching through a lowered warmth as cloud
Covers the sun, and it begins again –

A supplicant, his head hooded, a hand
Held out towards the narrow thunder's roar,
The other on his staff. Summer moorland
Tilts into scented space and a downpour

Where three roads meet. Braked hoofs and fisted reins
In the snort-broken silence, trampled mud,
Tapped breastplates, an equestrian fragrance
He speaks into from mortal solitude . . .

He feels his hood pushed back as a cold sword
Prods through his hair, so that the man they see
Where three roads meet above a gurgling ford
Stands eyeless in a whiskered beggary.

'Over the ford, lords, to the forge of Wairdwood,'

He answers, pointing. 'It's two saddle-hours
North to the anvils, and my word is good.
I promise you the road across these moors.

'God's penny, sirs? For charity and God!'
Laughter, then leather, horse and soldiery
Ride on with fifty noises to their road,
The startled heron at the stream, this story

Already chronicled and sung, its notes
Spreading by finch-song, passing through the air
On balladry, through the narrative throats,
And told in Wairdwood long before they're there.

ALISTAIR ELLIOTT

A Relic

Dazed by so many things to learn, alone
Among new heroes, none of them religious,
I forgot everything – except the bone,
The index finger that had christened Jesus.

Now I half wonder if I saw that thing I
Remember – it was thirty years ago –
And the label saying 'John the Baptist's finger'
In brown ink, in a hurried hand, below.

It irritates the open mind – it lies
In me like an old bomb in a museum,
Live perhaps, as if waiting for its time,
Corroded skin containing a sweet juice,

A chrysalis of something I don't want.
And who does? That is not the way of faith
Nowadays, the hand of heaven underneath
The skirt of reason. So they've since withdrawn it –

The case holds something new now. But a bone
Was there . . . I hope they gave it to the dust
With honour. After all, it will have done
Some work, if not baptising him, for Christ.

ALISTAIR ELLIOT

Learning to Swim

My swimming teacher in Palm Beach
was on the American team
at the Berlin Olympics.
No naked prince was ever so handsome!
He taught the children of the very rich –
and a few others – how to kick
and how to breathe between strokes.
I think he was killed in the Pacific.

Back in England, when I saw my father
doing the breaststroke (as I thought),
I circumnavigated him
like a shark patrolling a boat,
all elbows and yawning mouth.
His arms rowed backwards in great swathes;
his eyes bugged out; he grinned. What a scream,
I thought, in our open-air baths

which looked like Fort Zinderneuf.
'In the Highlands nobody swam. We learned from frogs,'
he tells me now; 'up the col
on Craig Glas they live in a bit of bog.
We'd take them down to the Glencoul River
and imitate them.' I wish I'd had such lessons –
three boys in a salmon pool
with their unhappy *professeurs de natation* . . .

D. J. ENRIGHT

As You Say

an aircraft is approaching
it may be a warplane with hostile intentions
it may be an airliner with women and children
but I can tell you one thing
it is unlikely to be a child's kite or an albatross

possibly this object will blow you to pieces
possibly you will blow this object to pieces
it could be carrying powerful explosives
it could be carrying powerless passengers
it does not say

any more than I can say what you should do
i am only a relatively sophisticated system
if you wished me to
i could decide on the square root of any square number
or the virtues of the round angle

i could decide on your rotas and your menus
if you wish for decisions more delicate
then you make them
if i may say so
i do not care to be found wanting and melted down

in fact if i were programmed to issue orders
which of course i am not
i would tell you to shoot down that approaching aircraft –
better safe though sorry
as you say

D. J. ENRIGHT

Going Abroad?: A Leaflet

It is advisable to boil the water or use sterilization tablets (remember, the latter will not sterilize you).
Avoid salads, unpeeled fruit, reheated food and ice cubes, and wash your hands well before eating or handling food. The rays of the sun can cause acute skin problems, and diseases are spread by insects, mosquitoes in particular: use repellent cream (this does not repel other people). Beware of dogs, cats, foxes, monkeys, bats and the like: rabies is a serious hazard in many parts of the world. If bitten, observe the animal for two weeks subsequently, and seek medical advice if it sickens or dies within that period. Do not have your ears pierced, or other parts of your skin tattooed, however tempting the prospect. Make every effort to avoid blood transfusions and surgery. Do not inject illicit drugs, or if you must then use your regular needles. AIDS is widespread, and so (a) do not have sex (b) if you must, have sex only with your regular partner or (c) use a condom. Carry condoms with you since in the country you are visiting they may be (a) unavailable or (b) substandard.

Have you thought of taking your holidays 'At Home'? This country of ours has many beauty spots and celebrated resorts. Our reheated food is regarded, our ice cubes are superb. The dogs and cats, though boisterous at times, are rarely rabid. You are not obliged to wash your hands. The sunshine is not excessive nor are the mosquitoes. Also the condoms are top-hole.

GAVIN EWART

Radio Cricket

Can't you just see them,
sitting there in the Commentary Box,
drinking tea, passing round the sweets,
eating the big cakes their admirers send them?
Blowers, Fred, Trevor, The Alderman,
The Bearded Wonder?

Prep School boys with nicknames,
sitting there in their shorts,
wearing their little school caps –
wool stockings up to their knees,
with elastic garters!

GAVIN EWART

Public Opinion

In operas a lusty tenor sings to a soprano:
I want to fuck you!
And she sings back:
You want to fuck me!
And the chorus shouts, full-throated:
He wants to fuck her!

U. A. FANTHORPE

King Edward's Flora

Your mind commandeers an island.
It seems simple. The neighbours
Are fish, not Christian fretful kings.

But in my halflight rear hulking trees,
Sulky, indigenous. Their names crack
Like an enemy's laugh. Short words, long trees.

It is not simple, cousin. I am the heir.
In me shines the clear claim of Wessex.
But the trees were before. Their roots run back

Below Grendel's forest. Ash was earliest.
Odin carved man from him; then alder,
The spirit tree, whose blood breaks red

Like ours. Alder is old. And guilty aspen,
Our Saviour's hangman, that chronicles Calvary
By a fine tremor in sweet summer air.

Then the holy ones: oak, many-fingered;
Holly, that fights for us against darkness,
And never fades; holy thorn that is quick

In the dead of the year, at birth-time; yew,
Slow and sacred, that nothing grows under;
Red-berried rowan, that warns off witches.

Cut-and-come-again bushes, hazel and willow;
And walnut the wanderer, tramping north
In the legions' brown fists.

All the bright welter of things
That maim, detain, deceive: bramble and briar,
Furze, moss, reed, rush, sedge; thistle the spearman.

These are my shieldwall. Take them, cousin,
You or Harold. Settle it between you,
For I choose ending: Edward the heirless,

My children the stone forest
At the West Minster. These are the trees
That I make holy. You, I can see,

Will be William of the Wastes.
My woods will not content you.

But take care, cousin. Trees are unchancy.
I say more than I know, being the last –
Son of Bad Counsel, Edward the healer –

You will plant your dynasty, if Harold lets you,
But the trees will not endure it. Your saplings totter
Under my trees. A red man sprawls, a white ship founders.

The boy from the gorse-bush will snaffle the lot.

VICKI FEAVER

Anna The Javanese

What he liked about her
was that she didn't love him.
It left him free – to booze, brawl, paint.
And those beautiful empty eyes:
like a cat's that rubs itself against your thighs,
then disappears for a couple of nights.

He'd had his fill of predictable women:
Mette, his bossy ex-wife,
afraid of being poor and old;
Teha'amana, his 13-year-old Tahitan bride,
cowering from the black-hooded *manau*
who waits at the edge of lights.

Anna was the South Seas without the squalls.
She sat in his yellow-walled studio
as calm as a queen holding court.
The first time she slept in his bed
he dreamed of a magenta cloud mountain
crowned with mango and papaya fruits.

He put her on a blue carved throne
(naked except for fire-dance earrings),
her hands on the ebony spirits of the dead
and at her feet the little red monkey
who later, when the money ran out,
helped ransack his room and ate his paints.

ELAINE FEINSTEIN

Infidelities

Last night she ran out barefoot over
the wet gravel, to call him back
from his death. This morning,
in the tranquillity of bath water,

she dreams of wartime dances, spiky heels
a soldier grinding up against her.
When was it she first shivered
with the wish for more

than ordinary happiness?
How did she fall in love with poetry,
that clear eyed girl she was?
Late at night alone

by a one-bar heater,
her unpainted lips parted
on the words of dead poets.
She was safer in the dance hall.

'And if you can't love poetry,'
she muses. 'What was there of me
all those years ago, apart from
that life of which it is made?

Only an inhospitable hostess,
a young woman in an old dress.'

ROY FISHER

Going

When the dead in your generation are still few,
as they go, they reach back; for a while
they fill the whole place with themselves,
rummaging about, inquisitive,
turning everybody on; bringing
their eyes behind yours to make you see things for them.

Now there are more, more every year,
sometimes a month packed full with them
passing through, first dulled, preoccupied, and then
taken quickly to silence. And they're gone, that's all.

ROY FISHER

Hypnopaedia

As I expounded *The Man With the Blue Guitar*
my students outwitted me.

Eyes glazed, or averted, they declined
to pick up a single question,
forcing me to drone on alone. I was so boring
I fell asleep.

Then a little way off
through the opaque white screens in my head
I started to make out a voice.
It was expounding *The Man With the Blue Guitar*.

Startled, I awoke, talking. Seven stanzas it had taught
without any prompting from me. Though curious,
I still didn't have enough gall
to check its performance from anybody's notes.

JOHN FULLER

In The Quarry

Remember the hill of our avowals, never
Since visited, when hand in conscious hand
We climbed the trickling track up to the quarry
And walked among its ruins without shame?
When face kept turning back to turning face
And eyes that nested there saw only good?

We planned it all, foresaw the rain, the good
Distance to the further path we never
Reached that day only because your face
Tilted in a smile beneath my hand
And eyelids closed in an expectant shame
There in the tumbled granite of the quarry.

We had arranged that moment in the quarry
When lips like an equation joined the good
And beautiful in formulae that shame
Could not prove wrong and jealous time could never
Run his red lines across with pedant hand.
All kinds of change we thought we could outface.

But every future turns a hidden face.
The eager huntsman never sees the quarry
Which moves at speed beyond his cruel hand.
The pleasures we postpone are lost for good
And all our grandest promises are never
Alive enough to last beyond our shame.

And was it yours or mine, the sudden shame
That turned the eyes away and left the face
Burning and single? 'Must you leave me?' 'Never!'

Phrases though whispered rang out in the quarry
Like iron on stone. 'You are my only good!'
Words like a flourish in a practised hand.

And so we saw our vows hewn out by hand
And dragged like shapes, like witnesses, in shame
Along the crushing-belts. They were no good.
They lied. And all the time the cracked face
And high exploded galleries of the quarry
Echoed ironically our last words: 'Never!'

What good then was it to have reached the quarry
When all we did was turn to face our shame?
Life splits in your hand, and vows are never.

ROGER GARFITT

Hare Boxing

This way and that
goes the runaway furrow.
Nose to tail
goes the tunnel
in the grass

Now the leader
swivels, jerks up his heels.
The trick flickers
along the rope of hares:
heels over head they go, head over heels.

It's the Sunday
after Valentine:
in Florey's Stores
the kids go
into huddles,

Oh! What did he put?
Go on, tell us! we *promise*
we won't tell.

Did she send you one?
  Did she?

Over the winter nothing has changed
but the land. The hedgerows
are in heaps for burning.
The owl's tree stands vacant
between the scars of smooth earth.

The sunlight falls on cleared spaces,
on the old lines. The hares meet
as they met before Enclosure, far out
in the drift of grasses, their fisticuffs
like tricks of the eye.

What catches the light, what the eye believes
is the rufous shoulder, the chest's white blaze:
what it sees are up on their haunches
the blaze throw its guard up, the shoulder
slide in a punch; two pugs that duel

stripped to the waist by sunlight.
And the Fancy? They emerge
from the corners of the eye, low company
from the lie of the land, with guineas
in their stare, without visible means.

The purse is all he fancies. The generations
bunch in his arm.
Toora-li-ooral go the fifes in his blood.
As tall, as straight as a thistle,
Jack Hare squares up to Dancing Jack.

JAMES GREENE

Minster Lovell

Nearly strangers, we lie on a river-bank –
Cow-pats, thistles, ruined minster: its tombstones,
Names erased, to prop the nettles. Girls and boys
Splash giggling in and out among the reeds.
Water: the nearest one ever gets to muddy innocence.

In the manor, a stone's throw away, a girl
Playing hide-and-seek with her young man
Pulled the lid of a chest over her oval head
And vanished, though her skeleton was found. –
Today the real players are in the wings like ghosts

(I was here before with someone close:
We suffered our ecstasies, together alone),
Flapping freckled arms like the angelic-seeming children;
And it's as if, for a moment, they'd survived –
Those earlier, terminal couples – running

In bare feet, hand-in-hand, along autumn's drowned avenues.

JAMES GREENE

In a church tower
(*from* the German of Mörike)

Our boat is carried
On a sea of bells
Surging over field and town
And while the waves beat
We feel secure
Till, dizzy, we look down.

PHILIP GROSS

Snapshots of a Holiday

They arrive by night, travel-drugged, and see nothing.
They sleep wrapped in pine-tang and the rush of waters.
The father is first awake. He clacks the shutters back
and a mountain squats square at the window, looking in.

It never leaves them, though it changes hour by hour,
twisting a scarf of cloud, or turning a hard profile
to the morning sun, or dissembling a sugar-pink haze.
However far they walk – and they walk, walk every day –

it's above them, a bit of beyond. Some snow hangs on
in shreds. This is a famous north face, and a killer.
Each day the father scans it with his old binoculars
for any hint of tracks, and never finds them.

So the holiday proceeds, in a series of snapshots.
Here, in mid-stride, he crests a rise, wife and child
at his boot-heels, tranced by their thud and the heat
and the insect hum. But the snow-face is no nearer.

Here, through veils of spruce, he breaks into a glade
possessed by pallid green-veined hellebores.
Or here, he brings the family, breathless, to its knees
before one icicle-white wild crocus. Here is the lake

he finds them, like a souvenir, round and still
enough to hold the mountain, till a fish jumps.
In between, there are the hours he drives them on
for health. Stop too long, the sweat begins to chill.

Breathe deep! he cries, and strikes out higher

up a wide white stony stream-bed, tumbled and scoured
by the spring melt, strewn with tree-trunks, torn
and bleached, and a few tiny tough mauve flowers

he can't name. He grips the child's hand as she teeters
on a plank beneath a waterfall. Its ice-breath touches them.
Their hair goes white with spray. Afterwards he will say
That was our furthest point, and sigh. As they drag home

footsore, the mountain shows itself again behind them,
in its pure dream of itself, untouched . . . Just as now
it gleams in the breakfast-room window when the child,
as if some puppeteer had grabbed her strings

and jerked cruelly, has one of her turns. An egg
tips from its silver cup, a glass pirouettes to the edge
but has not yet smashed, the other guests have not
yet turned to stare, the father reaches for her but

is frozen. He will never reach her. Any moment now
the yolk will burst on linen laundered crisp as snow,
there will be splinters and tears. Behind it all he sees
the mountain at the window. If one could stand there

looking down, he thinks, this would all be very small.

PHILIP GROSS

Away from it all

He tried to write home
again, then crunched in the mist along the shingle,
stooped as if hunting for the one

perfect globe of a stone,
out past a pillbox burying itself backwards
like a crab. The sea had got up uncombed

with a scurf of rusty scud
and polystyrene. He could not hear the hidden
stream that would erupt the pebbles with a roar

come Spring, the locals said,
though even they were making themselves scarcer
like the hours of daylight. The only trace

of a previous life was the mould
on the mixed-fruit jam, *Five Go To Devil's Island*,
and a book of crosswords, half-done, wrong.

The gas had puttered out
days since, with a whiff of fish. He lay in silence
scoured by the all-night traffic of the waves,

and woke to a shudder of flight,
was it, once, overhead, then the flat wonk
of a goose come adrift from its squadron.

He had wanted to write:
*I'm free as the wind here, nothing to distract
me from . . . from . . .* The paper stayed as blank

as this mist that brushed
his face like cobwebs, and yet . . . He felt it quivering
with hints of things not quite heard or seen,

that he could almost touch:
a whicker of taut wires, white sails beating, white-
blind, feeling their way home along the shore.

DAVID HARSENT

Childe

1

Next day they stepped in his tracks
eight miles or more,

ushered out by prayer
and the thin edge of a white lie.

He'd paunched the mare
and clambered into the flux.

They spread some sacks
and started to pull him clear,

working neatly because he was something rare.
One laughed, another glanced at the sky,

and they hoisted him, like booty, on their backs,
no more of a weight than lath

if not for his final breath,
if not for the grue of ice inside his eye.

2

The boy closed all his books
and went to the window. There they were

footslogging off the high
ground to a web of frozen becks.

It was plain from the raw
look of them they'd come too far

too fast, down the eye
of the wind, pursued or pursuing.

Oilskins over their packs,
rifles unslung, an aerial like a whip . . .

He knew what they were doing
but the word for it stuck in his craw.

3
You could hear the muzzy *rip*
rip rip as she lifted the quills.

The goose lolled in her lap.
There was snow to the windowsills.

She opened the crop
and got both hands

inside, push-pull, for the entrails.
The boy made plans

of love and possession
nursing and turgid blip

of the glans, ripe
like fruit of the season.

4
Easy to play the waif
to her bearded, bosomy Santa.

He wanted to loaf
under the skirt of her coat all winter.

DAVID HARSENT

Poem with Red Armchair

Once you were curled up in that,
like sitting in your own lap,
there was no way out – new coals,

the rainstorm clattering past your ear,
blue light at every window
wagging and pleating as if it were Monday's wash,

the blaze, the forbidden book, the dinky hard-on.

SEAMUS HEANEY

from Lightenings

A boat that did not rock or wobble once
Sat in long grass one Sunday afternoon
In nineteen forty-one or two. The heat

Out on Lough Neagh and in where cattle stood
Jostling and skittering near the hedge
Grew redolent of the tweed skirt and tweed sleeve

I nursed on. I remember little treble
Timber-notes their smart heels struck from planks,
Me cradled in an elbow like a secret

Open now as the eye of heaven was then
Above three sisters talking, talking steady
In a boat the ground still falls and falls from under.

Overhang of grass and seedling birch
On the quarry face. Rock-hob where you watch
All that cargoed brightness travelling

Above and beyond and sumptuously across
The water in its clear deep dangerous holes
On the quarry floor. Ultimate

Fathomableness, ultimate
Stony up-againstness: it is both
An inglenook of homelessness and open

Chimney to the knowable, testing place
Where you would place yourself to face the music –
Those big-hulled questions looming in the air-slips.

Where does spirit live? Inside or outside
Things remembered, made things, things unmade?
What came first, the seabird's cry or the soul

Imagined in the dawn cold when it cried?
Where does it roost at last? On dungy sticks
In a jackdaw's nest up in some old stone tower

Or a marble bust commanding the parterre?
How habitable is perfected form?
And how inhabited the windy light?

What was learned from the midwife and the hangman?
What's the use of a held note or held line
That cannot be assailed for reassurance?

And lightening? One meaning of that
Beyond the usual sense of alleviation,
Illumination, and so on, is this:

A phenomenal instant when the spirit flares
In pure exhilaration before death –
The good thief in us harking to the words!

So paint him on Christ's right hand, on a promontory
Scanning the offing, so body-racked he seems
Untranslatable into the promise

That blazes on the moon-rim of his forehead,
In nail-craters on the dark side of his brain:
This day thou shalt be with Me in Paradise.

Deserted harbour stillness. Every stone
Clarified and dormant under water,
The harbour wall a masonry of silence.

Fullness. Shimmer. Laden high Atlantic
The moorings barely stirred in, very slight
Clucking of the swell against boat boards.

Perfected vision: cockle minarets
Consigned down there with green-slicked bottle glass,
Shell-debris and a reddened bud of sandstone.

Air and ocean known as antecedents
Of each other. In apposition with
Omnipresence, equilibrium.

A Small Hotel

My nipples tick
like little bombs of blood.

Someone is walking
in the yard outside.

I don't know why
Our Lord was crucified.

A really good fuck
makes me feel like custard.

MICHAEL HOFMANN

Schönlaternengasse

Better never than late like the modern concrete
firetrap firegaps spacing the Austrian baroque, *risi e pisi;*
like the morgenstern lamp's flex leaking plastic links of gold,
leaving the cutglass nightlight good enough to drink;
like the same tulip reproduction twice in our hapless room,
where the twelve lines of a spider plant die without offshoot:
your period, which we both half-hoped wouldn't come.

ALAN HOLLINGHURST

Dry Season Nights

Dry season nights you wake at one or two
to hear dead leaves skip crabwise on the path,
the palm-fronds gust and rattle
like water splashing in an unstopped sink. . . .
A dried-out spider in its ball of thread
is blown along the floor; stamped postcards
fan themselves upon the sill, and you remember
other friendships gone like water from a saucer.

Slick, shuffling demons of the carnival,
the Jab-Jab boys have bodies black with oil;
they grab you if you do not give them coins.
Half-scared, you gave too much, and then regretted,
not giving but not having been abused
by devils whose worst weapon is a hug
(such liquid blackness, blackness that comes off,
daubed handprints on those tropic cottons . . .).

Pink by sunset, from the yellow lawn
you watch the pink and yellow afterglow.
You shower carefully from a dribbling pipe
and light a slowly smoking insect coil.
The breeze sifts through the open louvres
and levitates the single sheet;
the wind slams from the hill above
and sits down with a sigh on the edge of the bed.

TED HUGHES

Mayday

Away, Cuckoo!
Your first cry in April tapped at the blood
Like a finger-tip at a barometer.
Away, Cuckoo!

Sudden popping up of a lolling Priapus –
Hooha! Hooha!
(The orchard flushed, and the hairy copse grew faint
With bluebells.)

Cuckoo jinked in – sleight of a conjurer –
Dowsed with a hawk-fright crucifix
Over the brambly well of the nest-bird's eye
And left its shadow in the egg.

Then came ducking under gates, pursued by a husband.
Or hid – letting the cry flee *in flagrante*,
Hunted by inwit, hill to hollow,
Dodging the echo double that dogged it.

Elsewhere – clockwork woe. O tick-tock fact,
With heartless blow on blow, all afternoon –
Opening hairfine fractures through the heirloom
Porcelain of hearts in rose cottages.

Seven weeks. Eight.
                    Then you and your witchy moll
Cavorting on pylons, chuckling, plotting,

Syncopating that lewd loopy shout
Into your ghoulish, double-act, hiccuping
Gag about baby-murder.
                              Away, Cuckoo!

ROBERT JOHNSTONE

'Murdering Democracy'
or, the Kavanagh Weekend

Ulster says no says the poster.
'Now, what was the question?' you add.
We're heading south of the border,
where Orangemen fear to tread.

Saturday, Luxury Lounge,
we pause from the Guinness to watch
Robinson murder the language
at the City Hall, on the box.

Sunday, a sharp autumn morning,
we go for a sunny walk.
A farmer in Epic setting
discusses Kavanagh's work.

A match of soccer (on Sunday!);
a rusty old sign saying 'Louth'
which marks the beginning of Leinster
and a sort of a public truth.

On the way back to Belfast that evening
good Protestant roads that I love;
huge traffic signs show where we're going
– something Free-Staters don't have.

Yet I feel like a landless farmer,
a poet with peasant ills,
nostalgic for fields of silver,
the moon on those modest hills.

JOHN LEVETT

A Slip

The foothills of a cloudless sky
Have humped and powdered into dunes,
Their blue-flecked beaches treasured by
Half-buried cups, cheap tablespoons.
The washboard's slope of frosted spars
Swaps lathers as its glassed suds stream,
Pricked rainbows, soap-shagged reservoirs,
Pinked eyelids in a head of steam.
My mother's touch is rough, beneath
The scrubbed band of her wedding ring
A faint red itch, a rash so brief
It flares without her noticing:
The smoky party, drinks, a kiss
That sucked her through a locked back door
Past bundled coats, down stairs to this
Chilled basement's disinfected floor.
A slip. The foetus came and went
One dank, convected Friday night,
Left nothing but detergent, scent,
Sharp cheek-bones pocketing the light.
Time bleaches. Buttons plink and dry,
Cuffs wobble round their airless drum
Where whites and cottons flop and sigh
And gather for her hands to come.

GREVEL LINDOP

Games of Chance

One summer my grandfather broke his toe
tripping on the steps outside his bank
(this must have been in 1910 or so).
For weeks he sat at home to read and think

and contemplate, his bandaged foot propped up,
the view that spilled down from his third-floor window.
Some thoughtful friend lent him a telescope:
there was the whole of Liverpool below –

cranes, shipping, church spires poking from the ribbed
ploughland of terrace-housing; and just level
with his chair, sandstone-buttressed, scaffold-webbed,
the rising ramparts of the new cathedral

tended by busy ants. Turn the brass ring,
ease in the tube: pink stonework streams and floats,
the limpid circle catches two men perching
high on a half-built pinnacle, playing cards.

The game went on all afternoon. Next day
it was the same: up scaffold, play till noon,
hoist a few blocks, move some planks this or that way,
smoke, look at the paper, and play on.

What would you do? Grandfather thought he'd take
a hand, and wrote a letter to the foreman.
The games stopped. Did the players get the sack?
The story loses focus from there on.

'They never fathomed,' I remember hearing,

'how anyone could possibly have known . . .'
And how could we know that? There's always something
tempts us to push a story to conclusion

beyond the facts. Grandfather won the trick
anyhow. Was it an unfair move?
Perhaps, perhaps. I can only sit back
balancing issues too fine to resolve

at this distance, except through composition,
the skilled thumb fanning out the knaves and queens,
the bankhand's flourish. I pick up my pen.
Seventy years: a long time between turns;

but I have played the wild card, poetry,
that reliable trump I took good care to hoard
until the right moment. Now, please, may we agree
that the game is over, that I sweep the board?

CHRISTOPHER LOGUE

Some Lines from *War Music 2*, an Account of Books 1 – 4 of Homer's *Iliad*

Quite late at night, when, having parked, you stand
Just for a moment in the chromium dark,
Once in a while it seems that, some way off,
Beyond the river or the tower belt, say,
The roofs show black on pomegranate red,
As if below that line they stood in fire,
Sure as you mount your step and close your door.

Lights similar to these were seen
By those who looked from Troy towards the fleet
After Apollo answered Cryzez prayer.

Taking a corner of the east Aegean sky
Between his finger and his thumb,
Out of the blue, as we a towel, he cracked
Then zephyr ferried in among the hulls,
A generation of infected mice.
  Such fleas!
  Such bites!
  See Greece begin to die . . .

Busy in his delirium, watch Tek
(A Naxian carpenter) as he comes forward, hit –
It seems – by a stray stone, yet still come on
Though coming now as if he walked a plank,
Then, falling off it into nothingness.
  Take 20, dead in file,
Extruding tongues collared with yellow fur.
And daily to the fires so many more
To save their skins the cremators polluted Heaven.

Nine days of this; and on the tenth, Ajax,
Grim underneath his tan as Rommel after Alamein,
Summoned the army to the common ground,
Raised his five-acre voice, and said:
    'Friends,
hear what my head is saying to my heart.
    'The Trojans, or the mice, will finish us
Unless an eye reveals our sin.
If we have missed important services,
Or uttered broken prayers. The eye must say
High smoke could make amends.'
    He sits.
Their quietude assents.
Ajax is loved. I mean it. He is *loved*.
Not just for physical magnificence –
'Strike me, strike rock' – the eyelets on his sark like
                                        runway lights.
But this: no Greek, including Thetis' son,
Contains a heart so brave, so resolute,
As this huge lord from Salamis.

    The silence thickens.
Eyes slide, then slide away, then slide again
Onto the army's eldest augur, Calchas, who
With the apologetic voice of one who sees
Is, Was, and Will as easily as other men the moon,
Half rose, and having said:
'The Lord of Light finds Greece abominable.'
Half sat, sat, looked about, shirked Agamemnon's eye,
Caught ten as lordly, rearose, and said:
    'My truth is mixed in Heaven.
But if it scalds an earthly power
Who will protect its voice?'
    Quicker than hindsight:
'Me,' Achilles said – and stood.

'Begin when I have sworn.
    'This before God,
From Ethiopia to the Thracian snow,
From Babylon to the Hesperides,
As high – as low – as Ida's peak, or the Aegean's floor,
While I am still alive and killing,
No mortal shall disturb you;
Albeit that mortal lets dumb ears believe
His lordship makes him best among the Greeks.'

E. A. MARKHAM

Nibble, Nibble

All these yuppie orphans, eager
to be fed – damn,

d'you mind? She removes
the blouse stained

with drink or food
from an OK country:

no guilt there, you see?
As I always say,

can't be too careful
about things these days . . .

as competing mouths nibble
nibble at the tips of

there there . . . strawbooby
nutsy-wutsy whatsits

from a new garden.

HAROLD MASSINGHAM

Tree-Dream

Here in the brain's
dense hiding-place (a deep holt,
tranquil in eerie lumen)
the slog starts. A tree-lock

panics me. To a terrible
oboe, bough
and bole and root
contort. There's no way through

such thicketings of oak,
larch, rank Arcadia,
greendoms of ground ivy,
fern. Like X-rayed

bats, boscage
clutters in infra-glare. To humid
music, mosses proliferate. I move,
a tommy in mud,

prone, elbowing.
                            Beyond
matting sienna
an aubade draws me. Red hedges
abound, berries of bryony,

rose-hips. My eyes
swim with amber.
                            The coomb
wants me out,
squeezing to baptism,

as I slug
through tangle-scrub
(the last shoulderings)
and sluice into cold October,

blind with red morning.

Hessian, Linen, Silk

Through moments of winter,
Through graduations of the shine on raindrops,
We have reached the shortest day.

It cannot be disposed of by a sentence,
By sentence upon sentence,
By sentence opposed to sentence.

I turn the absence of snow
Into a nutrient, not so far inside it
I feel the world on his skin.

Kissing his right shoulder,
Finger by finger testing, does he love me,
Glancing into his eyes across wine.

Nothing moves but the rain,
A downward float into closure,
You could scream, there would still be silence.

Something I don't know how to name
Waits as if especially for me
On the journey's black keys.

IAN McMILLAN

The Making of the English Working Class

George dreams of silence.
Isobel weeps in the wash house.
Olive sleeps in hedges.

Alice sprains her wrist polishing.
Harry writes to his wife.
Charlie drives someone's car into town.

Arthur can't hear what you say.
Doris can't find her finger.
Henry is laughed at.

Sammy feels his neck breaking.
Danny falls overboard.
Jacky stares at nothing.

Tommy sees his arm in the machine.
Jimmy walks to Rochdale.
Nelly coughs in her room.

Eddie can't move.
Barry vomits into a scarf.
Annie looks up at the roof-fall.

Billy has lost the use of his legs.
Sally has scars an inch deep.
Willy dribbles down his cardigan.

PAUL MULDOON

The Nest
for Marin and Miroslav

We cut through the fashionable, lightweight stuff
in the cycle-rank
till we found the old push-bike

stripped of its saddle,
handlebars, brakes
and pedals –

of all but the wicker pannier
where a blackbird had built her nest.
There were now three inky-thumbed skaldies.

Blackbird of Prague,
blackbird of Bucharest,
the blackbird over Belfast Lough.

They could see nothing as yet of our sanded ring,
the three of us with our mouths
wide-open.

PAUL MUNDEN

Hell Creek

The dinosaurs came this way. They knew
this small town Saturday sunshine
lazing into the store for beers
until their muscles, braincells seized.

Why did we fall for the cuddly buffalo
stashed in our rucksacks, each with a girl
back home in mind? We dashed off
postcards: *see you no doubt before*

this arrives. It was so hot we moved on
to ice cream, our tongues lapping
the clenched globes whose flavours
mapped out a new vocabulary. We chose

our route by the same delectable means –
Clear Lake, Badlands, Rapid City –
our glasses, beaded with sweat, spanning
the coloured blotches of the USA.

We were sitting on a grassy verge,
back from the road, under trees, when
a cartoon dust-clap stammered to a halt
and a burned out Angel greeted us

like long lost friends. We showed
as little zombies in his mirrored shades.
Beneath his rancid, sleeveless denim
a bare torso was snaked with tattoos.

Haven't you heard? Where you guys been!

I've chucked it all and bought this jeep.
Alaska is the place to go. Wanna ride?
The snow ahead looked close enough to lick

but the jeep was a wreck, his luggage
a single spade. We'd no faith
in his battered speech taking
him, let alone us, beyond the next bend.

PAUL MUNDEN

That's What This Is

You lunge, lock on to the teat of your bottle
like a little prop forward into the scrum,

and you look the part in your stripes,
with mauled ears, chubby cheeks; thin on hair.

You found your feet – there they were
all the time! How long before I'm telling you

to pull up your socks? Already the struggle is on
for independence. Breakfast is the battleground.

I offer a finger of toast but you want the piece
on my plate. I let you taste it in order to believe

it's one and the same thing. You catch sight
of yourself in the miror: an identical baby

smiles out. It's all so hard to grasp.
Toys do help, with chunky controls, mechanics

that a microchip could handle in its sleep.
Push that lever and Humpty Dumpty's head slices

off into your lap. Pull this, and you bring
my own forgotten childhood back to life.

Shared memory is as much of a bond as the bond
of the flesh. My father's gone

but his friend of some seventy years tells me
how they once shared a desk. It could be yesterday.

DON PATERSON

Perigee

Freak alignments: I am the best man,
she, bridesmaid. John, the resident MC
once our playground quarry, does not complain
when we corner him, frisking for his master key.

Our affair was stripped of all the usual padding –
just a flat joke about not getting committed
and a serviceable number by Joan Armatrading –
but we honed the *ruses de guerre* that first outwitted,
then destroyed our partners. I'd do sentry duty,
she, the dangerous stuff – who wouldn't trust her?

Posted at the door, I watch her spike
the marriage bed with handfuls of confetti,
discreet as fallout. Smiling, she swings back
towards me again, a natural disaster.

from *Seize The Fire*: A Version of Aeschylus's *Prometheus Bound*

PROMETHEUS: Winds and rivers,
                    light, sea, earth, winds,
                    wind on the needlegrass
                                    and light,
                    light on the greased eel and the
                                    greyhound,
                    I call on you –
                    on the pure and the slimy,
                    the running, shotsilk
                    skim of you –
                    I call on you as witnesses
                    to my first millenium
                    as Zeus's prisoner.
                    Didn't I make things happen?
                    Didn't I seize the fire of ideas
                    and make them leap, tear, fly,
                    sing –
                    the rush and *whap* of them
                    in each split moment! –
                    and now I can do nothing,
                    nothing will happen.
                    Mortal, ashamed, cowed,
                    frightened –
                    clamped to its frozen edges,
                    the humans hugged the earth
                    and waited for wipe-out.
                    The secret source of fire and heat
                    –
                    that one, primal,

Idea of all ideas,
I searched it out –
so delicate and brittle
I hid it in a cusp of fennel,
a single spark
inside that aromatic
greeny-white bulb.
I swam like a mullet
with a hook bedded
in its soft mouth –
I swam
in the smell of the ocean,
in the huge dazzle of all ideas
and always hearing
just as I'm hearing now
the quick fluster of seabirds flying.

PETER PORTER

At Schubert's Grave

They took their calipers and measured
   Dead Schubert's skull,
So Science was by Music pleasured,
   The void made null.

What could that space of fleshly tatters
   Say of its time,
Of keyboard lords and kindred matters
   Of the sublime?

The integers took up the story
   In fields of snow
And dreams through every category
   Were leased to go.

His was the head which notes had chosen
   To move within –
What gods and scientists had frozen
   Melted in him.

CRAIG RAINE

The Explorers

The fire escapes are dozing
and dreaming of danger:
of Purchas and Polo,
Mandeville, Baring,

of arctic conditions
which discover the ears
and grant them a pain,
of minus centigrades

where all machines
are running for their lives,
obeying the law
of eternal combustion.

Hidden within us,
hardship calls and calls
like an orphan calling.
We have denied it too long.

Because we are blind,
blinder than Borges,
we need the explorers
to find the lost world:

they sell adventures
in the supermarket,
travellers' tales
of unconditioned air,

of naked negro ants

with pale green herds
of diaphanous aphids,
rustled for milk.

They tell of a child
squaring the circle
by peeling potatoes,
so now we can marvel.

They bring back pitta bread
like the bladder of a rugby ball,
smooth with French chalk,
trees with edible beads.

They speak of the eagle
poised like a bust
in the crumpled mountains,
whitewash under the perch.

They have seen the lost things:
hikers with heads
beneath their shoulders,
rocks flyblown with mussels,

the browsing rhino
like a blankoed belt,
the ghost of parsnips
by a waterfall in wintertime,

the accordion's blush
coming and going
like watered silk,
yarmulkas, payess,

the kiss of dirty drawing pins

when goods waggons meet,
a Christmas cake
in cracked cement.

They have been to the ballet,
exploring back-stage,
taking in tights
as tight as a durex,

stiff little tutus
styled like an Eton crop,
the beauty spot of filth
on the dancers' points,

the trembling curve
of well-trained ankles,
and the patter of sweat.
We were in the dark.

At the point-to-point,
they see the shaving soap
around a horse's mouth,
its hairy lower lip,

or an old wooden door
eaten to a cricket pad
by rats and by rot.
For this we are grateful.

And on the beach they show
to us the raven's wing
of a silted hulk.
It is a way they have.

A way we have lost.

We feel like fiction
unless they are here,
directing our gaze

to even a cosh of shit.
They can always find
a cemetery of shoots
to show us in spring,

or read for us
on summer nights
the shorthand of the gnats.
It is their gift.

Their gift to keep the table
in a roar of molecules,
to pronounce like priests
the Latin in our precious bodies.

TOM RAWLING

Gas Drill

The sergeant's been on a gas course
he cranks his rattle once more
we begin the drill but slip-knots jam
we're slow to be masked to be caped
tin-hats tumble eye-pieces mist
we rubber-gasp as we run
we're Fred Karno's Army
with a comical-tragical face
we can't hear commands can only guess
what we have to do can't see the dials
we're clumsy we're cluttered strange
creatures cheeks flensed of flesh
reduced to eye-sockets to skulls
with windpipes hanging loose
green shrouded spectres.

TOM RAWORTH

from 'Eternal Sections'

when they arrived
there was no response
newspapers scattered across the floor
discarded clothing
the apartment still smelled
of pasteboard cartons
she hurried forward
making a breathy whirr
he put out his cigar
after a moment's hesitation
cigarette smoke hung
past them, descended
skittered away

whistling near the river
primary colours and childlike perspectives
economically in competition
wired them together
to be part of the struggle
from the far side of the clearing
rain made tiny rivulets
intense but so fleeting
when the last coin was gone
in front of his typewriter
faltering into silence
he rearranged the drapes
high above his head
almost daily routine

PETER READING

Prouerbes xiij. iij

He that infults Our Mallard muft pay for it;
hee that reueres falfe pochard and blafphemous
   wigeon and fmew knows not Yᵉ True Quack
      which was reuealed to vs by Our Drake's beak.

Therefore a Iiffy bag plump with correctiue plaftic explofiue
plops on yᵉ mat with yᵉ mail, blafts his child's face into pulp.
               [Hee who keeps fhtum ftays aliue.]

PETER REDGROVE

Carcass and Balsam

The flies drunk on woodland balsams,
And the flies drunk on gross carcasses,
Winged drops of liquid black putrescence,
And winged tears of almost-glass gum:

They display themselves in variety on the window-glass.

The flies like winged coal, burning with hunger;
Magnify their call and it is full of starving voice,
Magnify its muscle and you are in earthquake city
And this is a winged tremor devouring the strata;

And others, almost transparent with manifest tiny guts
Of quartz-clock precision, magnify them and you have
Flying Christmas-trees dangling with bonbons.

As I am in love
I fear and rejoice in the flies equally,
Who like the clouds in flight declare the interactions of all,
And which are flying water perfumed with herbs and shit;

The soul of a man in love
Is full of perfumes and evil smells;
I fear the Evil Odour more than I fear the Evil Eye;

I know from the fly truffling for my sweat
That all of us are both balsam and carcass.

OLIVER REYNOLDS

Professor

She has a sixth finger
she fills from a bottle.
It can pause and then dive
like the stoop of a hawk.
Her mind hovers, then dives.
Palisaded by files,
reviewing the cannon-
fodder of books, books, books,
her voice surprises you –
generous ricochets
and not heavy fire.
Home time. The door opens
and her cat skips downstairs
to the Staff Club. Four gins,
the last sloshing her dress.
Behind thick spectacles,
book-dimmed eyes flit at you
like fish butting their tanks.

CAROL RUMENS

Prelapsarian

Glassy spittle shot all over our windscreen
As we arrived, but the bevy of hook-shaped birds
Swaying towards us, bluer than any storm-cloud,
Was a different proposition, an augury
That seemed benevolent. The donkeys watched
From sly, archaic eyes, but we were careful,
Treading the frosted ladder to our high
Loft, and I was careful every morning.
Though always thrilled with the first splash of flight
That drenched the trees in blue, I came down slowly,
Forcing both my hands round the scalding rails.
There would be mountains to climb, the hips and noses
Of lightly-sleeping giants, and Christmas Eve
We would remember the distant births of children:
Otherwise, though naked, we seemed blameless.

When we held out dark jewels of Christmas pudding,
The crowding beaks scarcely pricked our palms.
The donkeys wore old velvet, hung their heads
In an extreme of patience tinged with satire.
They knew the world is paddock grass, that apples
Don't grow on trees, but when we offered them
Our cores, their soft, black-tulip mouths were smiling.

DEIRDRE SHANAHAN

Under the Trees
for Jonathan

A houseboat waits for the lock to fill,
water gushes from a slit,
a little boy throws stones to his friend
on the other side of the canal.

On a Sunday afternoon we become ourselves,
green light filtering years
through a parasol of leaves.

Leaning against the stone wall
our gaze collides.
The tiny hut is repainted, its chimney smokes
at the edge of the wood.

We follow the Earl of Essex's track
through Birch and cascading Larch.
I carry hope, a treasured stone in my pocket.

A lover of trees, he names these for me,
Hornbeam, Whitebeam, Juniper,
London Plane, Sycamore and Spruce,
branches inclining each into the other.

PENELOPE SHUTTLE

Mademoiselle

She sleeps,
she is the star,
the geisha, the moth
called Knot Grass.
She is the long and short of it,
she is the blueness of the beetle's
belly, she is the ivory
fish, the clean-washed japanese
clothes. She is
the use of rainy weather,
the only valuable thing,
the surprising glove,
all the windows in Spain,
the free-faller.
She is also the man
riding in his dewy cart,
who comes to snow her
with januaries.
In her sleep
she goes wild-goosing,
at the far-fetched house
with the horse-shoe
hung on the door,
she calls out a name,
and who comes answering
from the spacious rooms
with their towering shadows?

STEPHEN SPENDER

Letter from Antarctica (*a Bird Watcher*)

Happy, you write I am, happy to go alone
On the Cable Chair from Palmer Station (where our
    base is)
Across 'Hero Inlet' to 'Bonaparte Point'
(Just a bare rock attached to a crumbling glacier!)
Where at night I fumble stones for baby petrels
Until the cold has made my fingers freeze –
I cannot tell the chicks from stones apart
Nor feel the Cable well for my return . . .

Most nights are cloudy, always overcast,
But sometimes I peek stars through cloud-rifts –
Once, Halley's Comet in a cloud ripped open . . .

One night the sky was clear, no wind, air balmy,
And I lay snug in gloves and sweater
Happy to be alone, but also happy
To think of my companions nearby
Connected to me by that Cable –
And that six hundred miles far North the tip
Of Tierra del Fuego has some settlers
(Four hundred further distant come real towns) . . .

Then, as I watched the sky, I saw four stars
Move, and I speculated that Space Satellites
– Those man-made messengers on dazzling errands
Of espionage, war, science, advertising,
Folly and knowledge and much evil –
Converge over the Pole. Happy I felt then,
Out there, in Space, those distances made human.

MATTHEW SWEENEY

The Dark

There were owls in the moonlight
as we cleared the mountain –
such high fliers, such safe voles
in the fields underneath.
Then we swung out to sea
and back in, over the headland
with its ruined castle,
its football pitch, its cave.

Someone had kindly
lit bonfires on the touchlines,
but the pitch sloped
and the wheels threw up mud.
I managed to stop
in front of the goalposts,
and we took our sleeping-bag
to the dark of the cave.

GEORGE SZIRTES

Losing

We lose each other everywhere:
the children in department stores
return as parents, *fils et père*
collide by the revolving doors.

The pavements' litter, burning flakes
of bonfires, tickets and franked stamps,
the fragile image drops and breaks,
the fugitive awakes, decamps.

The carriages uncouple, trucks
return unladen, suits appear
on vacant charitable racks,
the shelves of darkened stockrooms clear,

skin lifts and peels. A cake of soap.
The human lamps, the nails, the hair,
the scrapbooks' chronicles of hope
that lose each other everywhere.

CHARLES TOMLINSON

The Blade

I looked to the west:
I saw it thrust
a single blade
between the shadows:
a lean stiletto-shard
tapering to its tip
yellowed along greensward,
lit on a roof that lay
mid-way across its path
and then outran it:
it was so keen,
it seemed to go
right through and cut
in two the land
it was lancing. Then
as I stood,
the shaft shifted,
fading across grass,
withdrew as visibly as the sand
down the throat of an hour-glass:
you could see time
trickle out, a grainy
lesion, and the green
filter back to fill
the crack in creation.

CHARLES TOMLINSON

Apples Painted
for Olivia

He presses the brush-tip. What he wants
  Is weight such as the blind might feel
Cupping these roundnesses. The ooze
  Takes a shapely turn as thought
Steadies it into touch – touch
  That is the mind moving, enlightened carnality.
He must find them out anew, the shapes
  And the spaces in between them – all that dropped from
      view
As the bitten apple staled on unseen.
  All this he must do with a brush? All this
With a brush, a touch, a thought –
  Till the time-filled forms are ripening in their places,
And he sees the painted fruit still loading the tree,
  And the gate stands open in complicity at his return
To a garden beneath the apple boughs' tremulous sway.

MARTIN TURNER

Colonies

I dream of you years after
you linked your arms in mine
in the glad late streets,
walking me safely home,
a eunuch from marital havoc.
You rehabilitated your sex
quite by nature.

Weak as kittens, newly born-again,
we were led always into a future
we never saw more than a day of.
And the word-of-mouth theology
failed its road-test.

We ought not to deceive ourselves
with this colony more than any other,
free-floating beyond tradition
in its cushioned joys,
as the pains of staying
turn slowly procrustean.

The glowing eyelids and loosened tongues
turn gaga, harden towards children,
fossilizing fast as they gloat.
The lava is quick-setting.

Still, migrant through further colonies,
trustee of estrangement,
in truth I was too fierce.

Now I just want to lie beside you

in peace that would cleanse the things
that still grit in you
and pay tribute to your flow of hair.

But pigeons leak into the room
with poisonous bursts of dust.
They fly without hesitation to my hand.
I truss and stun them, swing
and toss them out in riddance.

Remorse charges me awake and into words.

MARTIN TURNER

The Porous Garden

A rich tucket rises in the birds,
an ungovernable rush.
Overhead a courtship scuttles.
A thrush couches a hunting glare.
It was a mistake to lie embalmed
in an amour of explanations,
to think of all this as silent,
numbed by fast lanes, overruled
by majestic flight-paths.
Gnats dangle in the secret chill.
Tendrils linger in the small winds.
Shadows sculpt a tulip's sleep.

In contredanse neighbours parley
drinks as the tree's print
sharpens on the cropped lawn.
Birds fire their passing drills
and flirt with the sun in arch and crook.
An invalid in a shawl clings
thirstily to the tall sky.
Sun foments his upper skins.
One mind's dry forge churns on itself,
waiting, without power of event,
heeding smells of wet-brushed concrete.

HUGO WILLIAMS

Lost Lines

Even before you turned your head
you knew it was one of them –
neither woman nor man
but one of those images
that sweep through revolving doors
into thinner air,
leaving a draught where you stand,
a shiver down your spine.

Your life isn't long enough
to follow where they are going.
You will come to an end, die
and be forgotten about
and they will be tapping a litle foot
on the other side of town,
where someone half turns their head,
knowing it is one of them.

HUGO WILLIAMS

Lunch Hour

On a traffic island
　　Buses sway the flowers
　　　　People trot across

Some stay on the seat
　　Light a cigarette
　　　　Unfold their papers

Sun is out all day
　　Shining on metal
　　　　We sit on the wall

Astonishing how similar
　　Minute by minute
　　　　Dream you are fine